NATANA

Natana

a novel

Mercedes Clarasó

BLACK ACE BOOKS

First published in 1993 by
Black Ace Books, Ellemford, Duns
Berwickshire, TD11 3SG, Scotland

Typeset in Scotland by Black Ace Editorial

Printed in Great Britain by Martins the Printers Ltd
Spittal, Berwick-upon-Tweed, TD15 1RS

A CIP catalogue record for this book
is available from the British Library

Hardback ISBN 1–872988–03–2
Paperback ISBN 1–872988–04–0

Set in PostScript Times
Using Telos Text Composition System TL4
Output through a Hewlett Packard LaserJet 4M

The publishers gratefully acknowledge subsidy from
the Scottish Arts Council
towards the production of this book.

My warm thanks for help and encouragement
are due to many; perhaps most of all to:

Medardo, who kept telling me
I ought to start writing.

Ilene, who has provided a guaranteed readership
of one for every word I have written.

Jean, who has helped with editorial advice
and other practical matters.

FOR MY SON, ALVIN

1

Natana wasn't all that fond of lifts. She decided she would walk up the stairs. After all, it was only two flights. When she got to the second floor she saw the name on the door right away. It's all turning out remarkably well, she told herself. No need to get all hot and bothered about it, after all. She was just about to slip the book through the letter-box when she realised there was a sound coming from the flat.

Someone must be hoovering, she thought, and paused, disconcerted. She had done her homework carefully, and knew that at this time of the morning he ought to be at work. She didn't really want to see him just yet, not till after he'd read the book. And then it struck her that perhaps it was someone else doing the hoovering. What if he'd remarried? If so, she felt she would very much like to see wife number three. Her curiosity got the better of her, and she rang.

The door was opened by a matronly lady wearing a wrap-over apron. There was a yellow duster hanging over one of her shoulders. Recognizing the insignia of the trade, Natana told herself she should have realized right away that it would probably be his cleaning lady.

'Yes?'

'Is this where Dr Locke lives?' A stupid question, she knew. After all, his name was on the door.

'Yes, miss.'

'Well, here's the book.' Natana handed it over.

'Thank you, Miss. I'll see that he gets it.'

Natana's smile had the added warmth that the excitement of the occasion had lent her. 'Thank you so much,' she said, and turned to begin her descent. As she heard the door close behind her she gave a great sigh of relief. Well, she thought, that's that. The die is cast. I am now committed.

Philip Locke had always assumed that he knew exactly who he was, what he was doing and why he was doing it. He was therefore slightly taken aback by this encounter with the inexplicable, or, at any rate, with what appeared to be inexplicable. He knew, of course, that there must be some perfectly rational explanation. It was just that, for some reason which he couldn't quite grasp, he had failed to perceive what this explanation was. Which was, of course, another example of the inexplicable. Philip was used to understanding things. He didn't at all enjoy the experience of being baffled.

My memory must be going, he told himself. He had no idea whether loss of memory was something to be expected at the age of forty-eight. On the whole it seemed to him this was rather early for this particular affliction. But things can creep up on one insidiously, he reminded himself. Like the grey hairs round his temples, or the tendency to sleepiness that he occasionally had to fight off now after a heavy meal.

Losing things, mislaying them, is, after all, a perfectly ordinary part of everyday life. Nine times out of ten it turns out that you've simply put the thing down in the wrong place, and don't remember doing so. Well, this was much the same sort of problem, only the other way round. The presence of this object that he simply couldn't account for was obviously just a different form of the same phenomenon. He must have got hold of the thing somewhere or other and put it down without paying much attention. No doubt someone must have lent it to him, for he would never have bought anything of the sort. And there it was, lying on the hall table. Since when, he wondered? Could he really be sure that the book hadn't been there when he went out in the morning? He knew he was not the most observant of men. It might well have been lying there for days.

After puzzling over it for some time he decided to seek clarification in the only direction that was open to him. He would ask Mrs Wells. It was just possible that she might know something about it. She was an observant and accurate lady, and would certainly have noticed the book when she was dusting the hall table. If nothing else, she would at least be able to tell him how long it had been there. For a moment the thought crossed his mind that perhaps it was Mrs Wells who had left it there by mistake, but he dismissed the fantasy with a smile of amusement. The possibility of her leaving behind any item of her own property in his flat was as inconceivable as the idea of her reading a book on the occult. Perhaps even the idea of her reading a book at all was equally out of the question. As for this one . . .

The Occult in Daily Life was its title. And the author's name was Savamindra, which struck Philip as peculiarly appropriate. So much so that he assumed it was probably a *nom de plume*. Overcoming his natural distaste for anything that savoured of the non-scientifically demonstrable, he had turned over the pages and found to his surprise that it was well written, in a correct and elegant style. He didn't read enough to be able to form an opinion as to the content. After all, he didn't need to. His opinion on such matters was already formed, and had been for many years.

Two days later, when Mrs Wells was due back, Philip left the house half an hour later than usual in order to be able to ask her about the book. One of the many excellent qualities Mrs Wells possessed was the ability to function independently, without his presence. Sometimes they didn't see each other for months at a time, but Philip knew that when he got home in the evening he would find everything in order, on the day she had been there. If any unforeseen circumstance arose, they communicated by note. Mrs Wells's notes were terse, not always accurate as far as spelling and grammar were concerned, but a model of clarity. 'Have replaiced washer in sink tap'; 'Front door creaking – have oiled'; 'Sorry, have broke yellow mug. Not valluable, I hope.'

As he wanted as much information as possible concerning the sudden appearance of the book, he thought he'd be better to communicate by word of mouth. With a little prompting on his part, he knew, he could get more information than would be contained in half a dozen of her telegraphic notes.

Mrs Wells was able to corroborate the fact that the book had only appeared on the day he had first noticed it.

'It was a young lady left it,' she added.

'You don't know who she was?'

'Never seen her before.'

'Did she say the book was for me?'

'Yes . . . or . . . well, no, I can't rightly say she actually *said* it was for you.'

'Can you remember exactly what she did say?'

Mrs Wells furrowed her brow in thought as she strove to recapture the exact words.

'First of all she asked if this was where Dr Locke lived. And then she said "Here's the book", and handed it to me. And so I never asked anything, thinking it was something you were expecting.'

'How odd! What was she like?'

'A very nice-looking young lady, she was. Very polite. Thanked me nicely for taking it.'

Philip wondered whether the term 'nice-looking' referred to the girl's manner or her appearance. Not that it mattered, of course.

On the whole he felt far from satisfied with the situation. It looked as if one mystery had merely been replaced by another. He now knew how and when the book had got there – handed in by an unknown young woman a few days ago. That was clear enough. He could now stop worrying about his own part in the affair. He hadn't been given the book and then forgotten all about it, or anything stupid like that. What he now needed was an explanation of who this young woman was and why she had handed the book in. For there was no question of her having handed it in to the wrong flat. She had specifically asked if this was where he lived. He had complete confidence in the accuracy of Mrs Wells' account.

Thinking about this, he found himself admitting with awe that he had never known Mrs Wells to be wrong about anything except spelling and grammar. He assumed that she functioned within a fairly limited range. But within her limits she was unimpeachable. The woman would make a wonderful witness. She noticed things, she remembered – he had never had to give her the same instruction twice – and she never digressed. A remarkable woman, really, he mused. But, in spite of his admiration for his domestic treasure, his thoughts wandered off to the other woman – the unknown, nice-looking young lady who had brought him a book on the occult.

That evening his friend Clive dropped in. Philip went to the kitchen to make some coffee and when he came back with the tray he found Clive holding the mysterious book between finger and thumb, as if he found it extremely distasteful.

'And what,' inquired Clive, 'is this unholy object doing in this temple of virtue?'

'You may well ask,' grinned Philip. 'I only wish I knew.'

'You mean, it just appeared?'

'More or less. All I can tell you is that it was handed in by a nice-looking young lady.'

'Some people have all the luck.'

'Not really. I wasn't in. It was Mrs Wells who received it. I never even saw the girl.'

'But she'll come back, surely. If for nothing else, to reclaim her property. And anyway, she'll want to know what you think of it. People who lend you books on the occult always want to know what you think of them. That's the only reason for lending them in the first place.'

'Don't you think that could be said about people who lend you books full stop – no matter what the subject?' To his surprise Philip found himself slightly on the defensive. He didn't quite like the implied criticism in Clive's statement. Whether it was the book or its donor that he wanted to defend he didn't really know.

'Ye-es, I suppose that does apply. At any rate, to the spontaneous offer of an unsolicited book. But it's peculiarly annoying in the case of a book on the occult, don't you think? It seems so superfluous.'

'You mean the lender should have occult means of finding out what you think of it?'

'Of course. The least you could ask, surely?'

'Here. Coffee's getting cold.' Philip handed the mug over to Clive.

'Right.' Clive took the mug and the hint. He got the impression that Philip was trying to change the subject, though he couldn't imagine why. But he certainly wasn't sufficiently interested to make an issue of the thing. 'Why, after all, should we waste time over a nonexistent absurdity, when we have the concrete delights of coffee to occupy us?' he said as he held the mug in both hands and sniffed appreciatively.

Philip wasn't paying much attention. He was thinking about Clive's suggestion that the unknown lender might come back and ask for his opinion. Perhaps, he mused, I really ought to read the book. It seemed ridiculous that he should actually be contemplating reading a book on the occult. In justification of the project he reminded himself that the book was after all decently written. Stylistically, at least, it wasn't the sort of rubbish he would have expected such a book to be. As for the contents, well, he could hardly hope to find anything greatly to his taste. But still, he felt he almost owed it to the unknown girl to be in a position to discuss the book, should she ever come back for it.

During the evening his thoughts reverted repeatedly to the little mystery. But he didn't raise the matter again with Clive. And that, he reflected after his friend had left, was odd. Normally he was in the habit of discussing with Clive whatever was uppermost in his thoughts. Why then, he wondered, did he feel this unaccountable but distinct reluctance to discuss this particular matter with him? There had been nothing uncharacteristic in Clive's attitude to the book. It was exactly what could have been expected of him – and of himself too. It was his own attitude that had veered from the established norm, and this was what had made him feel out of sympathy with Clive's dismissive reaction. Damn the book, he thought. It's affecting me already, merely by its presence in the house. Perhaps I'd better not read it, after all. You never know what it might do to me.

And then he reflected that this was a very pusillanimous decision to take. Nothing, he told himself sternly, could better convince him of the book's powerlessness to influence him than what Savamindra himself had to say. So he really must read the book. It was the least he could do to preserve intact what he regarded as his healthy scepticism. He was not unaware of the speciousness of this argument, and had to admit to himself that curiosity must certainly be playing its part in his decision. The fact that he should suddenly find himself anxious to read a book on the occult could only be explained by the mysterious circumstances of its arrival.

Clive noticed that his friend's attention seemed to be less keen than usual, and wondered about the cause. One of the things he most enjoyed about an evening spent with Philip was the fact that he could be relied on to miss nothing in the conversation. Any ambiguity, intentional or unintentional, any minor slip, any play on words or veiled reference, and Philip would pounce. But tonight the usual edge seemed to be missing. They chatted, that was all that could be said of the conversation. There was no sparkle, no illumination, not even a disagreement.

Clive left rather earlier than usual.

After he had seen his friend off, Philip went back into the sitting room, picked the book up from the coffee table where it had been left lying, and addressed it solemnly. 'Now,' he said, 'we'll see what sort of bedtime reading you make.' And he carried it through to the bedroom.

The two men had known each other since childhood, and their lives had run more or less parallel. They had gone to university together to study physics. Both had been seduced by the reputed glamour of scientific research, and had done their PhDs concurrently. After that, Clive went into university teaching while Philip took a job in industry which promised a future of uninterrupted research. At about this time both of them married, and both marriages ended almost simultaneously a few years later.

At this difficult time the two friends became almost inseparable, each supporting the other in his misfortune. They even discussed the possibility of setting up house together. But nothing was settled, and eventually Davina appeared on the scene. She took a good look at both men, liked both, and ended up with Philip. This put a certain strain on the friendship over the next few years, but they weathered the storm. Which was perhaps just as well, especially for Philip, since it meant that Clive was there to administer consolation, as before, when the second marriage broke down.

Lying in bed, now, with his unlikely companion Philip examined it carefully before reading the text, in search of any kind of clue as to its provenance. He had already looked to see whether the unknown lender (donor?) had put her name in it, but she had obviously preferred to remain anonymous. It had been published the previous year, by The Hidden Light Press. He didn't like the sound of that at all. Too esoteric by half. But he had to admit that the book observed the editorial decencies. It was well indexed, had a good bibliography, and even provided a glossary in which the uninitiated could look up the more abstruse terms.

Altogether, it was perfectly clear that this was not the work of an uneducated person. And this now became the most puzzling thing about the whole business. Even more difficult to understand than the book's unexpected appearance in his house was the fact that any book on such a subject could have been written and published according to the accepted canons of the literate. Up till this point it had practically formed part of Philip's creed that such books were only written *by* the ignorant *for* the ignorant. The readers he assumed to be universally credulous, the writers not necessarily so. In their case credulity had perhaps been replaced by cupidity. But, whatever the motives of the authors in question, there could be no doubt that this was the sort of thing that no educated man in his senses would dream of looking at.

Consequently he felt both guilty and uncomfortable as he finished his external examination of the book and began reading the text from the beginning.

'Occult forces', he read, 'shape our daily lives as powerfully and constantly as does the material world about us.' *Rubbish!* was his immediate comment. Each of the succeeding pages elicited similar exclamations of distaste. At the end of the first chapter he put the book down with a strong sense of satisfaction. He had found nothing in it to tempt him to change his stance on the subject. Knew it would be rubbish, he told himself as he switched off the light and prepared for sleep, with the pleasing consciousness of a good job well done.

When he woke up the following morning he had forgotten all about the book. He noticed it when he put his hand out to switch off the alarm. Bother, he thought, remembering that he had decided he really ought to read it, just to be able to discuss it with the girl. But why, come to think of it, did it matter whether he discussed it with her or not? And after all, she might not come. In which case he would have wasted quite a lot of his valuable time.

This idea left him with a distinct feeling of depression which he found a bit difficult to account for. Why should he care whether she came back or not? Why should he care about being able to discuss the thing with her?

No doubt, as Clive had pointed out, that had been her idea in leaving it for him. And it would be very nice to be able to oblige her. But, after all, the situation was not of his seeking. If she came back and found he had not read the book, she would hardly be in a position to complain. He considered himself a tolerably obliging sort of a chap, but he was a busy man. It would be unreasonable to expect him to sacrifice so much of his time for the sake of a total stranger, who might not even come back to ask for his opinion. And at this point the slight depression he had noticed before made itself felt once again.

He had a feeling he ought to try and investigate his reason for wishing to see the girl. Simply because Mrs Wells had said she was a nice-looking young lady? Don't be silly, he told himself. The world is full of nice-looking young ladies. What's so special about this one?

He came to the conclusion that the attraction must reside in the touch of mystery that this girl had surrounded herself with merely by her unaccountable action in leaving the book for him.

Why else should he care?

Even so, he thought. Even so. Granted that the spice of the unknown has its attractions, it was all the same a pretty low-grade type of mystery. The sort of thing he would normally think about for a moment and then dismiss with a shrug of the shoulders. Instead of which, he had read a whole chapter and was seriously considering reading more; perhaps even the whole book.

Philip came to the conclusion that his life must be very dull. Nothing else would account for his present reaction to the situation. He hadn't actually noticed that it was dull. But that in itself, the not noticing, was probably just part of the dullness.

Or was the dullness due to the not noticing?

He couldn't quite decide which came first. Not noticing things unquestionably led to dullness, and the reverse was equally true, and it didn't really matter very much which came first, except that if he knew that he might be able to find the origin of the situation.

At this point he happened to glance at the clock and leapt out of bed, abandoning his speculation. For the time being at least, dullness had been effectively banished.

Since the breakdown of his second marriage ten years earlier Philip had been living alone, and had worked out what he called a reasonable routine for the business of getting up, going to work, and seeing to his material needs when he got home in the evening. He had come to enjoy the little rituals he had established, and felt somewhat ruffled when anything interfered with them. He was therefore distinctly put out on this particular morning, when his reverie in bed had resulted in a thoroughly unwelcome rush. He was trying to eat his breakfast and finish dressing at the same time, hurrying backwards and forwards between kitchen and bedroom – and wondering whether all the extra journeys this entailed didn't perhaps more than make up for the time saved by combining the two operations – when his eye fell on the book, just as he was leaving the bedroom for the last time.

'Damn you!' he exclaimed. 'It's all your fault.' He crossed the room once again, grabbed the book and threw it into the wastepaper basket. He decided that the satisfaction he derived from this act of rejection more than made up for the few extra seconds involved.

He was still feeling disgruntled when he got home in the evening. Things hadn't gone at all well at work that day. The experiment he was most interested in just didn't seem to be coming up with the expected results. He checked his data again and again, grumbling over the waste of time this involved. In the end he came to the depressing conclusion that perhaps he was working on the wrong hypothesis. If so, that meant that weeks of hard work had been wasted. It was one of those days when he had quite a lot of administrative work to catch up on, and this always had a depressing effect on him. By the time he left for home he was feeling thoroughly frustrated.

This mood was not lightened by his remembering that he had left the house in a hurry, and so would not find things in their usual state of orderliness. If only it had been a Mrs Wells day, he thought. She always left everything in immaculate order, even on the odd occasion on which he had left a muddle behind.

A traffic jam of greater than normal proportions added to his frustration. As he sat fuming at the wheel, surrounded by a sea of other fuming drivers, he reflected that sitting in a traffic jam was probably the most senselessly damaging thing that modern man did to himself. He could feel his blood pressure rising as the minutes ticked past. I'll be at least half an hour late in getting home, he thought fretfully.

And suddenly reason spoke to him, in the midst of the discordant voices of his impatience and resentment. So what, it said. What are you going to do with that precious half-hour, anyway? You'll use it to do something remarkable with, will you? He found himself looking at his projected evening objectively, and had to admit that there was nothing, absolutely nothing, of any consequence on his programme. And he remembered his suspicion that morning in bed: that his life had become rather dull. Rather dull and perhaps rather pointless, he added now.

He got home at last, hot, tired and depressed, and set about putting things to rights before tackling the business of getting his evening meal ready. Then he stood for some time in front of the open freezer, but could think of nothing he could be bothered preparing. After that he performed the same ceremony in front of the fridge, but felt equally uninspired. In the end he made himself a sandwich and sat down in front of the television. But he didn't switch it on. He just sat and stared at the blank screen. It seemed a fitting symbol for his life at that particular moment.

Two days later he found *The Occult in Daily Life* lying once again on the hall table, with a note from Mrs Wells carefully placed on top of it:

'Found in bedroom waist paper basket. Was this Meant?'

2

At twenty-one Philip had had a clear idea of how his life was going to run. He had completed his first degree and was about to embark on his PhD. He had decided that this was to be followed by a lifetime of research, preferably academic. That was the model his father had set him, and he could see nothing wrong with it. In good time he would marry a woman of similar tastes and accomplishments, and they would settle down somewhere near his friend Clive Bowen, who, it had been decided – initially by Philip – was also to marry.

The idea was that they should live close enough for their children to play together, just as he and his brothers and sisters had played with the Bowen children. He liked the idea of order and continuity embodied in this programme, and, once he had explained his project to his friend, Clive had no difficulty in falling in with the scheme.

So far things had gone smoothly, and in accordance with the plan. And for the next few years they continued to do so with obliging accuracy. Life seemed pleasantly predictable. The whole concept of tragedy and disaster struck Philip as a useful fiction – without which literature would be remarkably flat. But there was no place for such upheavals in the life of a sensible man who had decided what he wanted out of life and was prepared to take the necessary steps to achieve this end.

Still according to plan, both friends fell in love as they neared the end of their studies, and married as soon as they had completed their theses. Clive had not held any rigid views as to what sort of woman he wanted to marry, so his choice brought no surprises. But it was at this point that Philip found that real life and his carefully laid plans diverged considerably.

The woman of similar tastes and accomplishments (with a good educational background and a respect for the scientifically demonstrable) no doubt existed. And had he looked long enough Philip would presumably have found her, and in due course fallen in love with her, as outlined in his plan. But the one thing he had failed to take into account was the arbitrariness of love. He had read, and thought, a great deal about the tender passion, and was looking forward to experiencing it – had, in fact, begun to look around him with a view to finding the right woman, when he suddenly realised he had already found her, and that she was quite different from what he had expected.

Mad as a hatter! had been Philip's verdict on Elise after they had first met. Crazy and affected, and probably stupid too.

He and Clive had been invited to a party to celebrate the engagement of another friend. Philip arrived before Clive and wandered about for some time, seeing few people he knew, feeling bored and slightly awkward, and consequently looking rather more lordly and imperious than usual. As soon as he saw Clive he went up to him.

'I say, Clive! Have you noticed how young all these people look?'

'Hmn, yes, so they do. Must be undergraduates, most of them.' The word 'undergraduates' was uttered in the slightly pained tones proper to the research student who had nearly completed his PhD, when referring to lesser mortals.

Almost at once Clive was dragged away to meet someone, and Philip found himself alone again.

But not for long.

He noticed a very pretty young woman coming towards him, holding a rose in front of her, almost at eye level, and gazing at it reverently. The rose was pale pink, with golden edges, and it occurred to Philip that the girl was much the same. Her long golden hair framed a face of delicate, almost other-worldly beauty. She walked right up to Philip and then stopped, holding the rose between them. Only then did she take her eyes off the flower and look up at Philip.

'Don't you think that beauty is everything?' she asked.

He was bitterly disappointed. Just as he was telling himself that he had never seen such a beautiful face, and that he would be happy to spend the rest of his life looking at it, the pretentious vacuity, as he saw it, of the words, completely broke the spell for him.

Angry with the girl for letting him down, and with himself for caring, he allowed his lips to curl faintly in the expression of polite scorn which he had carefully cultivated for use in the debating society, and answered:

'Not really.'

He was astonished at the effect his words produced. The radiance suddenly disappeared from the girl's face, she uttered a quiet little 'Oh!' of consternation, and he could almost have sworn that he saw tears welling in the blue eyes. Then she looked down, down past the rose, down to the floor.

'I'm sorry,' she said. 'I got it wrong.' For a moment she looked as if she were going to offer him the rose. Then she shook her head and turned away.

Philip looked about him and saw one of Clive's sisters standing near him, talking to a young man. Without apologising for the interruption he went up to her and asked urgently:

'Who's that? That girl with the rose over there?'

The girl was just about to leave the room, but Julia caught a glimpse of her in time.

'Oh, that's Elise. Elise Edgeworth.'

'Is she . . . is she quite right in the head?'

Julia laughed. 'Perfectly, I can assure you. Quite a bright girl, actually. A bit eccentric, if you like.'

'I certainly do. Never seen anything like it. Is she playing at being Ophelia, or something?'

'She's not playing at being anything. That's just what she's like.'

'Mad, you mean.'

'No, just natural.'

'Don't give me that! Nobody behaves like that naturally.'

'Not in our society, perhaps.'

'Well, she's in our society, isn't she?'

'Yes, but not of it – not entirely, anyway. Her mother comes from one of the Western Isles. I forget which.'

'There you are, you see. I told you there was something queer about her.'

'You didn't. You suggested she wasn't quite right in the head, which is rather stronger.'

'Yes, and probably a bit nearer the mark. Anyway, having a mother that comes from the Western Isles is no excuse for behaving like a deranged tragedy queen.'

Julia turned to the young man who had been standing patiently by during this exchange. 'What on earth can Elise have done to him? You'd think he was out for her blood.'

'I just can't stand that sort of affectation,' Philip said, and felt this was a perfectly adequate explanation for his attitude.

He went home almost at once, asking himself what indeed Elise had done to provoke such intense disapproval in him. Not that disapproval was foreign to his nature. Like most intelligent and thoughtful young people he had come to certain conclusions about the world and how to behave in it, and found it hard to believe that anyone else could give equal thought to the important issues and yet not come to the same conclusions as he had.

But, considering the brevity of their verbal exchange, he couldn't understand why Elise's words should have filled him with such wrath, especially when he had been so well disposed towards her. Had he known a little more about human nature he would have realised that it was precisely because he had been so well disposed towards her that he minded so much. If she had even said something trite, or dull, it wouldn't have mattered at all. He would have put up with the most ordinary of platitudes. After all, you can't expect such a stunningly beautiful girl to start off the conversation with a remark about Einstein or a reference to nuclear fission. That would have been an unreasonable expectation, and he considered himself a reasonable being *par excellence*. He had not expected of her anything more than the average. Simply to look into those eyes while she talked about the weather would have been a blissfully rewarding experience.

But to be asked to subscribe to the palpably false and ridiculously pretentious statement that beauty is everything! And then for her to react the way she had, merely because he had disagreed! The more he thought about the brief conversation, the more uncomfortable he became, and the more he felt obliged to exaggerate the girl's offence. By dwelling on the idiocy of her opening question, and the bizarre nature of her reaction, he kept at bay the need to examine his own part in the exchange. Otherwise he would have been obliged to admit that his response had been unfriendly, not to say positively boorish.

And anyway, what did she mean by saying she'd got it wrong? Was she implying that he looked like the kind of twit that talked that sort of drivel? At this point he got up and strode over to the mirror. 'Do I look like a bloody aesthete?' he demanded angrily. The young man he saw in the reflection was reassuringly square. The hair was short and well groomed, the clothes totally unimaginative, the features pleasant but unremarkable. He found himself still staring at his reflection a minute or two later. Why did she have to pick on me? he wondered, and could see nothing in the mirror to explain the choice.

He sat down again and tried to dismiss the incident from his mind, without success. Gradually he found himself thinking more and more of the distress that his reply had obviously caused her. And she had apologised, she had said she was sorry, she had even tried to give some sort of explanation, with her:

'I got it wrong.'

Perhaps he had been a bit hard on her. Perhaps he could have distanced himself from her extravagant ideas with a little less brutality. He suddenly remembered his mother's much repeated warning about how hurtful his scornful manner and cutting words could be. 'That may be the way to win an argument,' she would say, 'but it's also an excellent way of losing friends.'

By the following morning he had come to the conclusion that he must do something about it. He simply had to apologise. The first part of the programme was comparatively simple. All he had to do was get hold of her address and write or phone. He knew he would be able to get his information from Julia, perhaps even from Clive. The more difficult bit would be the question of what to say to her once he had established contact. But he would cross that bridge when he came to it. First of all he had to find out where he could get hold of her. He was to see his friend that morning, and he would start off by asking him.

He had some difficulty in deciding what he would tell Clive, for he must give some reason for wanting to get in touch with the girl. He didn't feel at all happy about revealing the true reason. The more he thought about it the less he liked his part in the affair. But he was in the habit of speaking frankly to Clive, and didn't like the thought of not being straight with him. And a respect for the truth was something that both his nature and his education demanded of him.

To his surprise, as soon as they met, Clive handed him an envelope, saying Julia had asked him to give him it.

'Julia?' said Philip, in some mystification, looking at the dainty pink envelope. Not at all the sort of thing he would have expected from Julia, who was a down-to-earth, no-nonsense sort of a girl. This little missive looked far too assertively feminine for her.

He opened it and took out a fragile little sheet of paper, almost transparent in its delicacy. There was no heading, and no signature. But at the foot of the page was a drawing of a rose. Very simple, very uncluttered. Just a few elegant pen strokes, and there stood the rose. The words were perhaps a little less easy to interpret.

'I'm sorry – again. But this time it's to say that I think I did get it right in the first place. Can we try again?'

'Well, I'll be blowed,' he exclaimed in his surprise.

'What is it? What's that sister of mine up to now?'

'Nothing. It's not from her.'

Clive looked at him inquiringly, wondering whether he was supposed to ask who then it was from.

Seeing his look, Philip held out the note to him.

'Looks like you've been having an argument with a rose,' was Clive's comment, as he returned the note.

'That's rather what it feels like too. Do you know a rose called Elise?'

'Elise Edgeworth? Yes, she's a friend of Julia's. Nice girl. A bit – original, shall we say?'

'Yes, I think that's quite a good way of putting it.' And Philip told Clive about the previous evening's encounter . . .

'So you see, I was going to ask you where I could get hold of her. I really do think I owe her an apology.'

'I can give you her address all right. But look, I think I'd better warn you. She's not a very rational or practical person. After all, just look at this note. No signature, no address. How does she expect you to get hold of her? That's the sort of thing I mean.'

'Well, she managed to find out how to contact me. She must have given me credit for an equal amount of intelligence, that's all.'

Clive looked sceptical. He had a feeling that his well-meant attempt at interference had come too late.

Philip phoned Elise and they arranged to meet the following day in a little café of her choice. While waiting for her he had a good look round, and thought the place was very strange indeed. Most of the customers seemed to be students, but he would have guessed they were art students, or perhaps from drama school. All the walls were covered with posters announcing meetings or activities of a somewhat esoteric nature. Meditation, mouth music, weaving, folk dancing, poetry readings – all were on offer. There was a genuine mediaeval shawm for sale, equally genuine Chinese chopsticks, a choice of saris. For those seeking enlightenment there was a talk on Zen as well as a series of lectures on Celtic mythology.

Philip felt rather uncomfortable in these surroundings, and had just decided gloomily that Elise would probably be half an hour late when she appeared; remarkably punctual. Later he learned that this punctuality had cost her a considerable effort, but that she had felt it was essential in the circumstances, in order to show him that she was a perfectly reasonable being who could behave like any normal person.

'I'm so glad you decided to give me another chance,' she said as soon as they had sat down. 'I made such a mess of it last time, didn't I?'

'We both did. I'm sorry, I know I was rude.'

'No, no. It was all my fault. *I* was the one who got it wrong.'

'Look, I really don't know what to make of this. First you said you'd got it wrong. Then, in your note, you said you'd got it right. And now you're saying you got it wrong after all. Do you think you could explain the whole thing, from start to finish, very simply and clearly, as if I was a child of rather limited intelligence? I just don't think we're on the same wavelength at all.'

'Oh, but we are, I know we are. That's the bit I got right, the moment I saw you. I knew it right away. And I asked several people about you, till I found one that knew who you were. And it was after that when I made the mistake. After all, I had just found out you were a scientist, so I shouldn't have taken it for granted that you understood about the power of beauty.'

Looking at the clear, earnest eyes in front of him Philip suspected that he was beginning to understand now.

'But the rose,' he said, still sufficiently his own man to want to get his facts properly assembled. 'Where did the rose come in?'

'I brought that with me. From my mother's garden. I meant to give it to you.'

‘But when you left home you didn’t know you were going to meet me!’ he objected.

‘That’s not why I brought it along in the first place.’

Philip felt a slight stab of jealousy. ‘Who was it meant for, then?’

‘Oh, nobody. I just brought it along for company.’

‘Company? I’d never thought of a rose as companionable.’

‘They are! Very. So are most flowers – not zinnias, though. And that’s why I didn’t give it to you after all – the rose, I mean. I felt so low when you rejected me that I just couldn’t bear to part with it. Was that very selfish of me, do you think?’

Philip assured her that it wasn’t. He made the statement with great conviction, thinking of the embarrassment that such a gift would have caused him, and the inevitable ungraciousness of his acceptance – or perhaps even refusal. To his surprise he found himself making an effort to silence the part of his mind that was still trying to run the conversation according to the rules he knew and understood. He felt as if they were talking in a foreign language which he couldn’t possibly understand but yet somehow did. It was an extraordinarily exhilarating sensation.

But habit persisted, and he made a renewed effort to clear up some of the remaining mysteries in the situation.

‘Look, you said you thought we were both on the same wavelength.’

‘I said I *knew* we were.’

‘How on earth could you possibly know – when we hadn’t even met?

‘I don’t see that our having met has anything to do with it.’

‘With actually knowing we were on the same wavelength?’

'Yes. And that's why I wanted to meet you.'

'But don't you see you've got things in the wrong order? The meeting must surely come before the knowing.'

'Why? I don't see why it should be in that order. And in fact it wasn't.' She spoke gently, trying not to ruffle him, but with absolute certainty.

'But . . . but how did you know? How could you possibly know?'

Elise was beginning to look a little distressed under this interrogation. 'How does anyone know they know something? It's not a thing you can explain. It just happens. How do you know you like that coffee you're drinking?'

Philip nearly replied that he didn't really like it at all, but stopped himself in time. He didn't want to give her the impression that he was criticising the place she had chosen for their meeting. Besides, whether he liked the coffee or not was irrelevant, and the rational part of him reminded him that one at least of them must stick to the rules of logical discourse. But when he tried to find an answer he found himself on rather shaky ground.

'I know I like it . . . because . . . because my taste buds tell me. Everything we know or perceive comes to us through one of our senses.'

'All right, then. It was one of my senses that told me we were both on the same wavelength.'

'Which one?

Elise thought for a moment, then looked up triumphantly. 'My sixth sense, of course!'

'Of course,' said Philip, gently mocking.

But Elise missed the note of mockery in his voice. She looked up, smiling happily. 'There! I knew you'd understand.' And she held out her hand to him.

Philip was touched, and took the little hand between his own, holding it tenderly. He was so thrilled by the contact that he managed to ignore the fact that he had just agreed, tacitly it must be admitted, to the existence of a sixth sense.

Suddenly it seemed to him that there really was nothing to argue about. It was surely much more important to find out all he could about her, and he began asking questions. He learned that she was an only child, that she had refused to go to university, thus incurring her father's displeasure:

'I didn't want to spend three years of my life reading dusty old books. And Daddy said I'd never get a decent job without a degree, but Mummy knew better and encouraged me to try for this job in a boutique, and I got it, and so I spend all day among beautiful things. Isn't it wonderful?'

'What sort of beautiful things?'

'Crafts and pottery and silk scarves and folk weave skirts, and things like that. Oh, and prints, some wonderful prints. It's really a lovely way to spend your time, among beautiful things all day.'

Philip remembered her offending statement about beauty being everything, and realized that in her case it was not a matter of affectation. Beauty, it seemed, was her creed. He saw how grossly insensitive he had been, and blessed her humility and persistence, without which he would probably never have seen her again.

She told him that her mother came from the Hebrides, and that it was a wonderful, wonderful place, but that her father's job in banking kept them in London, and that her mother did nothing but dream of going back to North Uist. 'Isn't it sad? Why can't they both have what they want? Why can't they both be happy?' She looked at Philip with a troubled expression. 'You know, I sometimes think no one is really happy, and it makes me so sad.'

'*I*'m happy,' he stated with complete truth. 'I don't think I've ever been so happy in all my life.'

'I'm so glad,' she sighed. 'That completely restores my faith.'

'Your faith in what?'

'In everything.'

Philip went home much later than he had intended, wondering what they had put in the coffee. He felt elated, excited; astonished. Everything he saw looked unique, full of value and meaning.

He stood on an overpass looking down on the traffic below and marvelled at the intricate play of its progress. It was as if a divine hand were guiding the cars on their way in a precise and predestined pattern. He imagined that each car was trailing a brightly coloured strand behind it, and tried to visualise the superb tapestry that this apparently random piece of weaving would produce. The fact that he thought of it as only apparently random can be seen as a measure of the alteration to his normal state of consciousness.

When he got home he put his hand on the garden gate to push it open, and noticed its colour for the first time. It's green, he thought, and it struck him that there was something particularly wonderful about having a green garden gate. He closed it with care and walked reverently up the garden path, while waves of undirected tenderness flooded over him.

'You're late,' said his mother. 'We didn't wait.'

'I'm sorry, it's just that I . . . '

'Yes, I know, dear. You just wanted to get that chapter finished, or something.'

'Yes, well, something like that,' he said, resisting the temptation to grab hold of his mother and waltz round the room with her. He wanted to tell her, he wanted to tell the whole world; only he wasn't quite sure what it was that he wanted to tell.

How could you possibly explain a phenomenon like Elise?

'Look, darling,' his mother was saying, 'you know I don't want to interfere with your work, but I sometimes think you're overdoing it a bit. After all, you've just about got your thesis finished, so what does it matter if it's a week or two earlier or later? You know you've plenty of time.'

He tried to convince his mother that he wasn't working too hard, and had no intention of doing anything of the kind. At that moment the thought of working on a thesis seemed a highly absurd thing to do. He wondered how he had ever brought himself to spend the last three years doing it.

Mrs Locke was left unconvinced. She realized her son's behaviour was not quite as usual, and could only attribute the change to overwork. She was therefore all the more surprised when, towards the end of the evening, she heard him playing the piano. Haven't heard him play in years, she thought. And that piece of all pieces! He always hated *Für Elise*. Said it was the worst thing Beethoven ever wrote.

3

Nearly a quarter of a century later Philip had quite forgotten the ecstasy of being in love with Elise. After the breakdown of his marriage he had done his best to wipe out all recollection of those heady, bewildering days. And he had succeeded to the extent that Mrs Wells's words, 'Was this Meant?' had failed to evoke any memories of Elise and her conviction, obdurately held in the face of all the evidence against it, that things were indeed Meant in this life. He simply had a good chuckle over the question, and made a mental note to tell Clive.

As for the book . . . Thinking the matter over, he came to the conclusion that he had thrown it into the wastepaper basket in a fit of misdirected pique, simply because he was annoyed at himself for having got up late. The book, he now decided, was not so much culprit as scapegoat in the little early morning drama. And his argument for reading it in order to be able to discuss it with the girl, should she ever reappear, still stood. Not only did he want this discussion to take place, but he realised it would seem pretty spineless to have to return the book unread. Surely it was up to him, as a thinking man, to be in a position to refute all its false arguments and ridiculous claims. No, he really owed it to himself to read the book.

That evening, however, instead of settling down to get on with the reading, he went over to see Clive. After his wife's death Clive had refused to move out of the suburban villa they had bought near to the one Philip and Elise had settled in. The choice of houses had been made in accordance with the prearranged plan of their student days. They were close enough to visit each other frequently, and for their children to play together. But both couples had remained childless. At one point it looked as if Clive and Myra at least would fulfil their part of the bargain. To their great joy, Myra became pregnant after several years of marriage. And then she contracted leukaemia, and within a few weeks Clive had lost both the unborn child and his wife.

In spite of pressure from friends he refused to leave the house. The very reason they gave against his staying seemed to him the best possible argument against moving. The house was full of memories of Myra, and if all he could have were the memories, then he would have to make do with them. He certainly wasn't going to give them up. His happiness had been far too short-lived for him to be able to part with any fragment of it. For though the marriage had lasted nearly four years, the happiness had been of much shorter duration.

Clive had not been in love with Myra when they married. He had married her more or less as both he and Philip had planned to marry – out of common sense, a desire to found a family, to follow the traditions and customs of their class, to re-enact their own happy and secure childhood. Myra was a thoroughly nice girl – pleasant, intelligent, perhaps a little stolid. Clive had thought it would be a good idea to marry her, had spoken to her on the subject and discovered that she felt much the same about it. All seemed to be going well. Both sets of parents approved, so did his brothers and sisters; so, more importantly, did Philip. Myra was the very prototype of the woman Philip had had in mind. Philip too was about to marry, and even if his choice had strayed considerably from the pattern originally intended, at least they all liked Elise, and in all other respects things were working out as planned. Suitable jobs had been found for both young men – a lecturer's post for Clive, a position on the research panel of a large aeronautics firm for Philip.

There seemed to be no clouds on the horizon.

And yet, as the wedding dates approached, the attitudes of the two young men diverged. For Philip the wedding day was to be the beginning of eternal bliss. For Clive it began to assume an increasingly threatening appearance. He could find no way of accounting for this. Myra was a dear, her family was lovely, their position in the world was going to be all that could be desired. And yet as the wedding date approached Clive's spirits sank lower and lower. Myra of course noticed, and, sensible girl that she was, tackled him on the subject and offered to release him from the engagement. But the thought of letting her down, when he realised that the trouble was not in any way of her making, was more than he could face. What reason, what possible reason could he give to her, to the world at large, for not going ahead with the marriage?

He tried to discuss the matter with Philip. But at this point Philip was living on a plane on which rational discourse had no part. It was not till two years later that Clive understood the role that Philip and his euphoric state had played in his own sense of distress. And it was in fact Myra who had been able to explain the matter to him.

In nearly everything Myra was the opposite of Elise. Dark and stocky, with more character than beauty in her face, her mind worked in a completely different way. No intuitive leaps for Myra, no comforting, irrational convictions. When Myra had a problem to solve she would spend a long time collecting all the facts and poring over them till she was convinced she had all the relevant material. Then she would set to work on them, examining them from every possible point of view, weighing them up, checking that she had no false information, fitting the facts into whatever pattern she could make of them.

And after two years of studying her husband's unhappiness, she came to the conclusion that the real trouble stemmed from the contrast between his matrimonial lot and that of his friend. For Philip, love and marriage had been a total transformation, a reversal of the natural order of things, a revelation of a new world, inhabited and irradiated by this exquisite, other-worldly creature who had taken him up and carried him off to share with her the joys and mysteries of Elfland. For Clive marriage had merely been a prolongation of his previous, settled existence. No revelation, no shocks and no thrills; no great new vistas. Without the example of Philip's happiness all might have been well. Clive might never have come to realise that it was possible, perhaps even desirable, to live in hitherto unknown mental and emotional regions.

After she had discovered what she thought was the cause of Clive's misery Myra still had to solve another problem. Did Clive understand the reason for his unhappiness, or was the poison working underground, below the level of his conscious mind? It was the fear that Clive did understand the situation that kept her from attempting a discussion with him. They were not close to each other in any way except the physical. Even their lovemaking was more in the nature of a duty than a pleasure. Each feared to deny the other this token of union. Each feared that the other might take amiss any refusal or apparent lack of interest. And so they made love, punctiliously, each in ignorance of what the act might mean to the other partner.

So Myra was left wondering whether to communicate her discovery or not. For if Clive had found this truth out for himself and said nothing about it to her, it was surely a sign that he didn't want to discuss it. And if she were now to attempt a discussion of the subject he might object to having his chosen privacy violated. He might even take it as some sort of complaint on her part. And Myra, unhappy as she was, had no wish to complain. She knew that many men, faced with a marriage that no longer appealed to them, would have jumped at the chance she had given him of backing out. That he had not done so she attributed entirely to his sense of honour, and felt grateful for it, in spite of the fact that the marriage had brought her no happiness either. For how could she be happy when she saw the daily proofs of his depression and lack of zest?

The one point that Myra and Elise had in common was a great humility. It never occurred to Myra that she too had a right to happiness, and that if Clive understood the source of his misery it was his duty to discuss it with his wife and see if there was anything that could be done about it, for her sake as well as for his own. And so she pondered over her discovery for many weeks, afraid to bring it into the open and cause possible offence. The last thing she wanted to do was give Clive the idea that she was complaining. He had quite enough to worry him as it was, poor lamb!

She dithered on for a long time. And then one afternoon she went to see Elise and found her in tears.

For a long time Elise had seen the signs of Philip's gradual descent to the world he had inhabited before meeting her. She was so convinced, as he had been, that their meeting had brought to him a new dimension in life, that at first she refused to acknowledge these signs for what they were. She would find all sorts of reasons to account for his growing indifference, his tendency to pick her up on any of what he called her airy-fairy statements, his increasing unwillingness to admit that the world was a wonderful place, ruled by wise beings who saw to it that things would always turn out right.

Elise simply couldn't understand the change.

After all, he had seen things her way. Ever since their first conversation in the café he had told her, and told her with rapture, that she had shown him a completely new and beautiful way of looking at the world. Why should anyone who had seen this truth want to change? How could anyone who had seen this truth stop seeing it?

But one day, after she and Philip had spent the previous evening with her parents, her father had rung her up from his office and told her, with a certain amount of satisfaction, that he could see that his prediction was coming true.

Mr Edgeworth had had his reservations about the marriage, and had told Elise from the start that he was convinced that the differences of belief and outlook were far too great.

'But, Daddy,' she had pointed out, 'that's not the case any longer. I know that at first he saw things in a very rational, materialistic way. But he has agreed, fully and freely, that all this has changed. He says I've opened the eyes of his soul. Isn't that beautiful?'

'Yes, dear. Lovely. But that's because he's in love with you. Love can do some pretty queer things.'

Ignoring the second statement, Elise pointed out that there was no reason why he shouldn't stay in love with her. She at least would give him no cause to stop loving her.

'No, my dear, I'm sure you won't. It will be quite unnecessary. I'll give you two years.'

Elise had looked at her mother, and both women had exchanged a smile of conviction and complicity.

And now her father had brutally pointed out that his prediction was coming true. 'I even got the time right,' he gloated. 'Two years, that's what I said.'

Elise was filled with grief on a number of points. Her father had put into words the very fears she had been trying to shake off for some time. He had also hurt and astonished her by the vindictiveness of his action. Why did he have to tell her that her marriage was foundering? Simply for the pleasure of proving he had been right?

And then it struck her that this whole sad game had been played out once before, many years ago, between her parents. For the first time it occurred to her that perhaps her father had known only too well what he was talking about.

But her mother, then? Why had her mother taken the view that all would be well with the young couple, if her own marriage, an exact parallel, had brought nothing but unhappiness? Was she perhaps hoping to redress the balance by a happy marriage on her daughter's part? Elise had known all along that her mother had not been happy in her marriage. But she had attributed this to the fact that her husband's job kept them in London, while she pined for her Hebridean home.

Elise had spent the rest of the day in tears, weeping over two generations of unhappy marriage. Myra's arrival made her try to pull herself together. But after a few moments of forced conversation her grief burst through once again, and she confessed all her unhappiness. Myra in her turn told her about the problems she too had to face, and they ended up agreeing that marriage was not quite so simple and not quite so blissful a state as they had imagined.

Before leaving, Myra turned to Elise and said, 'Do you mind if I tell Clive about your problems?' Seeing that Elise looked slightly hesitant she added, 'I think it might help a bit with my problem.'

'In that case, yes, of course. But perhaps they've both discussed it already. At one point I thought I knew every single thing that Philip thought and felt and said. Now I'm not sure I know any of it.'

Myra left with her feelings in rather a mixed state. She was sorry about what was happening to Elise and Philip. But on the other hand she now had her starting point for the discussion with Clive. Now at last she felt she was in a position to act.

'I went to see Elise today,' was her introduction to the subject that evening when Clive came home.

'Really? And how did you find her?'

'In tears.'

This statement produced the desired effect. There was no trace of the former indifference in Clive's next question.

'What on earth was the matter?'

Myra explained, then asked whether Philip had said anything about the domestic situation.

'No, not really. But I could see he had reverted to his usual more rationalistic way of looking at things, and I wondered what effect this might have on Elise. A bad one, it seems.'

'Bad and sad. And I've mentioned it because I think it may have some bearing on our problem.'

'Our problem?'

'The fact that you're so unhappy. Which leads to the fact that I'm every bit as miserable.'

This was the first mention of his unhappiness that had been made between them since their discussion before the wedding. Clive stared at his wife for a long time in silence, and Myra stared back.

'I didn't know you knew,' he said at last.

'We discussed it before we were married, and you'd never said anything to make me think things had improved. And I can see they haven't. And I think it may all have something to do with those two. The fact that they were so happy, that

Elise had given Philip such a completely new outlook on life. Whereas I gave you nothing.'

'Oh, Myra, how can you say that?'

'What I mean is that I gave you nothing that you didn't already have. Elise gave Philip a world full of romance and mystery. I could do nothing like that. And I think that's what you've been missing. If it hadn't been for those two you would never have known that there was this wonderful new dimension you were missing out on. And once you were married to me there was no hope of . . . of anything of the sort. I can't lead you into fairyland.'

'Well, perhaps fairyland isn't the right place for an adult human being anyway. It looks as if poor Philip has found this out.'

'And poor Elise. I think she'll have to come down to earth. Or lose Philip.'

After this conversation Clive began to notice his unhappiness slipping gradually from him. In its place he found an increasing admiration for Myra, an admiration that soon turned into love. When eventually they discovered that she was pregnant they felt that their happiness was complete. The misery of their first two years was lost in their present happiness and in the expectation of the joys of parenthood. He became convinced that the satisfactions of founding a family and having a loving and greatly loved wife were far beyond any happiness to be found in an excursion into fairyland. And more lasting, he thought, certainly more lasting.

More than twenty years later Clive was thinking yet again of the irony of this naive assumption and of the bitter way in which all their hopes had been defrauded with Myra's sudden death, when Philip arrived.

'I've come to talk about the occult,' he announced.

'I hope you're better informed on the subject than I am, for I know nothing about it except that it's a load of rubbish. I take it you've read that book?'

'The first chapter. And it has done nothing to make me change my mind.'

'In that case, what more is there to say? Why talk about it?'

'Because I'm still fascinated by the mystery of the thing. Of the book's arrival, I mean. Sooner or later, I hope, this mysterious young woman is going to come back and claim her own. I'd just like to have some idea of who she might be, and of why on earth she's left me the book in the first place.'

'Why come to me? I know as little about it as you do. How can I help?'

'I just thought that if two trained minds were brought to bear on the problem we might come up with the right answer.'

'But even if we did, we wouldn't know it was the right answer till the girl comes back. If she ever does.'

'Of course she'll come back.' Philip spoke with a touch of irritation. 'It was you yourself who said she would. She'll want to know what I think of it.'

'Well, yes,' agreed Clive. 'That's what any rational person would do. But the mere fact that the book is on the irrational—'

'The occult,' interrupted Philip.

'Same thing.'

'Not necessarily.'

'I say, that must have been a pretty powerful first chapter!'

'Don't be silly. I simply meant that there are lots of irrational things that have nothing to do with the occult. It's a matter of distribution, to use the technical term.'

'All right, all right. I thought you were actually implying that the occult isn't included in the irrational.' There was a slightly amused smile on Clive's face as he spoke the words. He couldn't help feeling that Philip was reacting rather defensively on behalf of the book, and found this both puzzling and entertaining.

'Anyway,' he went on, 'let us by all means find a probable explanation for the entirely improbable.'

'It may be improbable, but it is a fact. So come on, explain it. For a man who spends his time explaining the laws of physics to the élite of our youth the problem should not prove insoluble.'

'Jehovah's Witnesses,' stated Clive. 'It's their latest ploy for gaining access and softening up the victim. By the time the Witness actually turns up you're so intrigued that you're prepared to listen.'

'Hmn! Not very convincing. Try again.'

'Well, the obvious one is that it's just a raving lunatic.'

'I don't see what's so obvious about that.'

'The subject of the book predisposes one to think along those lines. And the behaviour, you must admit, is unusual, to say the least.'

'You can hardly equate unusual behaviour with raving lunacy.'

'All right. You try, then.'

'Perhaps it's an advertising gimmick. New way of promoting sales.'

Clive was shaking his head. 'It would work out too expensive. Think of all the man hours it would involve – or rather, girl hours. But how about this? There's this gorgeous bird who has seen you somewhere and fallen madly in love with you. She's desperate to strike up an acquaintance and pops the book in as a sort of conversation starter.'

'But why a book on the occult?'

'I suppose the only answer to that one is: why not? How was she to know you're intelligent as well as good looking?'

Philip ignored this.

'Look,' Clive went on, 'the whole thing is probably some sort of a joke. At least, it might be. But then, it might not. Might there not be something more serious, perhaps even slightly sinister, in the thing? How do we know you're the only person to have received a book in this mysterious way? Perhaps it all forms part of an organised attack.'

'By whom and on whom?'

'By some occult sect or other. That should come to light when you've read the whole book. And it may be aimed at intellectuals in general. How's that for a theory?'

'Hmn! Perhaps. But in that case it should have been you, as a university professor, who got it. First thing they'd do, surely, would be to aim at the academic establishment.'

'I see you're not going to be satisfied with any of my suggestions. But you must admit I've tried. Have you no other suggestions of your own?'

Philip shook his head. 'I just wish the damn girl would come back and explain. I hate mysteries.'

'Yes, neither of us is very good at not knowing. It sort of makes you feel you're being got at, doesn't it?'

'Yes, it does, sort of.'

Philip went home quite early, determined to get on with his reading. But when he got back all thoughts of reading were driven from his mind for some time by the discovery of a note thrust through the letter-box.

One sheet of primrose yellow paper, and on it the words: 'I came about the book. Sorry I missed you. I'll try again next week. Natana.'

The matching envelope had his name on it, Dr Philip Locke. That was all.

Damn and blast, he thought. Why does she have to come when I'm out? He strode about the flat for a while in a state of extreme annoyance and frustration. He seldom went out in the evening, so why did she have to choose this one to turn up? He was annoyed at her, at himself, at Clive. After a few moments he sat down and told himself to stop behaving like an idiot. After all, she had said she would come back next week. He took some comfort in this, till he realised that this was only Monday. That meant that it would be at least a week before she came, perhaps nearer two.

Still, he was at least in a much better position now. He knew she would come back. And he knew her name. Natana. An unusual name. He'd never come across it before. Beautiful, though. It sounded foreign, but he couldn't make up his mind as to what language it seemed to belong to. Was the girl herself foreign? He examined the note again, looking for clues, but had to admit to himself that she was giving nothing away. The English was perfect, and totally free from any personal characteristic. Simplicity and clarity, these were its only qualities. And if she were foreign it would probably have shown in her accent, and Mrs Wells would certainly have mentioned it if she had noticed anything of the sort.

After a while it struck him that there was one possibility that neither he nor Clive had thought about. All along they had assumed that the book had been handed in by a perfect stranger. Why had it not occurred to either of them that the girl might perhaps be someone he knew? Probably because of the subject matter. He couldn't think of anyone he knew who might have an interest in the occult. But having thought of this possibility he now began to wonder whether he had met this girl somewhere, at some point.

He began a mental review of all the young women he knew, slightly hampered by the fact that he had no idea of what limits to set on Mrs Wells's interpretation of the word 'young'. He was beginning to realise that the quality of youth, for him at least, now extended much further than it had a few years ago. Ten years ago, he thought, I'd not have described a woman of thirty as young, and now I certainly would. And Mrs Wells must be sixty if she's a day. That means the 'young lady' may be forty, or forty-five, for all I know.

He sat down determined to review the whole list of all the women he knew who could possibly be described as young. Friends and colleagues, wives of friends and colleagues . . . With a start he realized he must also include daughters, and meditated on his own inconspicuous but relentless passage from one generation to another.

Try as he would, he could think of no woman of his acquaintance who could conceivably have left the book for him. And yet this new idea, that it had been left by someone he knew, stayed with him. He told himself that, if he had ever met a girl called Natana he would most certainly have remembered the name at least, if not the woman. And yet the idea persisted, the almost-conviction that, somehow or other, and contrary to all probability, there was some personal connexion between him and the girl.

This is ridiculous, he told himself suddenly. I've spent practically all evening on this stupid problem – first discussing it with Clive, and now . . . He picked up the note and re-read it yet again. Then he phoned Clive and told him about the latest development.

'If I hadn't come to see you I'd have been here when she called, and by now I'd know what it's all about,' he pointed out.

'You're not complaining, are you? After all, if you'd been at home you'd have been caught out, with most of the book still unread. You've been given a week's grace. I suggest you get on with the reading, since it seems to be so important to you.'

Philip felt slightly ruffled when he put the phone down. He didn't at all like the way Clive had pointed out how important the incident had become for him. The fact that he had realized this himself before phoning didn't help in the least. He felt sure that his interest in this unknown girl was affording Clive a certain amount of amusement. 'Idiot,' he said out loud, not quite sure whether the epithet was directed at himself or at Clive. Almost as if he thought I was in love with her!

He decided to dismiss the whole matter from his mind and get on with some of his own reading. There were always lots of other things piling up, waiting to be read.

Before sitting down he went over to his cassette cabinet to choose some background music. Bach, he decided. That's what I need. Order and clarity. He sat down and closed his eyes for a few minutes, listening to the Goldberg Variations. Yes, that was it. Order and clarity. Problems posed and then elegantly solved. He picked up a book dealing with the borderline between physics and philosophy.

Half an hour later he had to admit to himself that his concentration was not up to its usual standard. It's that damned book on the occult, he told himself. The whole thing's really got me unsettled. I'd better just get it out of the way.

He picked up T*he Occult in Daily Life*, and was about to start reading at the beginning of the second chapter, when the name Natana floated into his head.

Natana, *Natana*.

Really an exquisite name. It struck Philip that he had read the first chapter rather superficially. If he was going to make any sense of the rest – assuming there was any sense to be made of it – he'd really be better to start again from the beginning. After all, as a scientist, he knew it was dishonest not to tackle things with an open mind. Besides, if he was going to convince Natana of the error of her beliefs, he must make use of all the ammunition that the book no doubt provided. That, after all, is the advantage of having a trained mind, he thought.

Natana . . .

4

With one of her intuitive leaps Elise suddenly realised that she had found the right name. Savamindra, she thought. That's it. I shall write under the name of Savamindra. It sounds absolutely right. Just the one name. No one will even know whether I'm a man or a woman. Savamindra – the perfect name, with something of oriental mystery to it.

The more she thought about it the more she liked her choice. Even the different components of the name seemed just right. The first two syllables reminded her of the French savant – learned, yes, that was just right. The idea of learning was precisely what she wanted. And then the next syllable, that was perfect too. Mind, which was what the book was all about. The learning of the mind. That just left the last syllable. Ra – oh, of course, the Egyptian God. Splendid! Not that there was anything specifically Egyptian about what she had to say; but the presence of a god, of whatever nationality, in her new name seemed wonderfully apposite. All the gods are one God, she reminded herself. Yes, Ra would do beautifully. How opportune that this simple, monosyllabic version of the name of God fitted so well into the word that had suggested itself spontaneously to her. It would have been a bit difficult to envisage a name into which she could have fitted Jehovah, or, say, Jupiter.

She was in one of her mercurial moods, having a quiet little laugh over her far-fetched etymological explanation of her new-found name, and at the same time convinced that this Savamindra that had come to her so effortlessly was indeed the right name to work under in her earnest enterprise. From now on, she said to herself solemnly, I shall *be* Savamindra. This is how I shall think of myself. This is what I shall ask all my friends to call me.

By the time she had found her name the book was already well under way. She had made copious notes over the past few years, she had organised her material so that she knew exactly what each chapter was to deal with, and had worked out how the different parts were to fit together. She had even done more than half of the actual writing. And that part, to her surprise, had turned out to be much easier than she had expected. She blessed her painstaking education for giving her such a good grounding that expressing herself correctly on paper was never a problem. And she was deeply thankful for the ever-gushing fount of enthusiasm that sustained her from start to finish.

This enthusiasm came from two different sources. There was her lifelong conviction that the unseen is more real, and much more important, than the seen. And then there was her longing to be able to make some form of reparation to the man she had walked out on all those years ago. She had to admit to herself that it was perhaps a bit naive to suppose she could reach out to him by means of the very thing that had proved the stumbling-block in their marriage – her own unshakeable belief in the reality of the spiritual world. She still remembered with excruciating clarity the first occasion on which she had realized how fundamentally opposed their viewpoints were.

The first year of their marriage had been an enchanting, poetic adventure. She sang the songs of the Hebrides to him, told him the sad, weird stories her mother had brought with her from her remote island, and Philip listened, enraptured, allowing himself to be carried along in the shining stream of the Celtic imagination. At first he never stopped to ask himself whether he actually believed all this. It was enough that he was floating in this magic world with Elise by his side. But gradually his lifelong mental habits began to reassert themselves. He found himself smiling indulgently at some of Elise's more unverifiable statements, unwilling to say anything that might break the spell. Unwilling even to *think* anything that might break the spell.

Philip had for some time been trying to hang on to his convictions as well as to the enchantment of Elise's magical view of the world, when her father precipitated the first overt hint of dissension. The Edgeworths were spending the evening with their daughter and her husband. Mother and daughter were greatly attached to each other, and were always very happy when they were together. This happiness showed in the greater volubility displayed by both women. They talked and laughed, sang snatches of song, exchanged recipes, admired each other's clothes, and spoke at length of all the far-away members of the family, living out their misty lives on their remote island.

The men looked on, smiling, pleased to see the women so happy. At least, that was how it seemed to Philip. But when both women were in the kitchen Elise's father took the opportunity to say, 'Of course, as a sensible man, you don't believe all this nonsense they talk, do you? I mean, Great Aunt Deborah's second sight, and the curse hanging over the Black Well, and all that.'

'No, of course not.' It was the first time Philip had ever been forced to ask himself bluntly whether he, as a sensible man, really did believe all this. Up till then he had been content to drift along, lost in the spell which Elise had spun round him, living in this new world and still managing not to think too closely about its relationship to the world he had been brought up in.

The women came back from the kitchen, and Mr Edgeworth made no further reference to the matter. But for the rest of the evening Philip found himself wondering just how much he could allow himself to believe in some of the subject matter of the conversation. And from that day on he was questioning his position constantly. It seemed to him that he had betrayed his scientific training and beliefs. And he thought of the expression with which Clive and Myra had sometimes looked at him, and it reminded him of the indulgent yet sceptical way in which Mr Edgeworth looked at the women of his family. Was it possible that Clive and Myra were laughing gently at him for going along with Elise and her airy beliefs? He became increasingly conscious of the split within him. He still felt the pull of the new, more intuitive way of looking at things. But at the same time he felt ashamed of the fact that he was condoning beliefs that he could find no rational way of justifying.

Up till then he had merely allowed a slight scepticism to slip into his share of the conversation, as when they were talking about their projected summer holiday, and Philip suggested a date for their departure.

'Oh, no! We can't go that day. It's a Friday.'

'What about it?'

'It's unlucky. We can't travel on a Friday.'

'But, my darling, thousands of people, tens of thousands of people, will be travelling that Friday. Is it unlucky for them all?'

'It could be. Especially if there are all those thousands of them. That's simply asking for trouble.'

Philip was defeated by this combination of the superstitious and the practical. They travelled on the Saturday, along with not tens, but hundreds of thousands of other people.

Nothing untoward happened to them, apart from troublesome delays, and Elise took the opportunity of pointing out to Philip that their accident-free arrival was due to the fact that they hadn't travelled on the Friday.

'But my darling, all those other people did travel on a Friday, and nothing happened to them. So it would have been all right for us too.'

'Not necessarily. Two more might have made all the difference. You can't prove that nothing would have happened if we'd been there simply because nothing happened when we weren't.'

Philip laughed. 'Unanswerable,' he said, and kissed her.

It was this use of logical thinking in the service of the fanciful that both delighted and baffled Philip. He began to wonder whether perhaps the situation required a little rectification. All the winning cards seemed to be in Elise's hands, thanks to her ability to switch from one plane to another. Philip decided that, as the thinking member of the partnership, it was up him to make some effort to define the boundaries a little more clearly. Fact was one thing, and fancy was another, and he had nothing against their intermingling; but he felt it was incumbent upon him to make sure they both knew which was which at any given point in the conversation. And, having made this decision, he then proceeded to do nothing about it till spurred on by his father-in-law's words.

On the morning after the parental visit he made his first unambiguous stand in defence of the rational. As they sat at breakfast Elise was reading a letter from a friend in Stornoway. When she had finished she put it down with a little sigh.

'That was from Mhairi,' she said. 'Her mother's just died.'

'Really? What was wrong with her?'

'Nothing.'

'My dear Elise, you don't die, just like that, if there's nothing wrong with you.'

'But there wasn't anything wrong with her. She went to bed one night feeling perfectly all right, and the next day they found her dead in bed.'

'Heart failure, I suppose.'

'If you must put a label on it. But then, all death is heart failure,' Elise pointed out.

Mastering a slight feeling of annoyance Philip took refuge in a conventional expression of regret. 'It must have been a great shock for the family.'

'Not really. She knew it was going to happen and she'd warned them.'

Philip put his cup down with visible patience.

'And how did she know, might I ask? You've just said she was perfectly well.'

'She'd had a message two days before.'

'A message? What sort of a message? From whom?'

'Oh, just a message.' Elise waved a hand vaguely in the air. 'From beyond.'

Remembering his conversation with his father-in-law the previous evening Philip decided he couldn't in honour let this pass. After all, he had assured the older man that he didn't believe any of this nonsense.

'Well,' he said, assuming a benign expression, 'it's a very nice metaphor.'

'Metaphor? What do you mean, metaphor?'

'A metaphor is a figure of speech whereby you say something is what you know perfectly well it isn't, just because of some similarity.'

Elise shocked him by her reaction.

'Christ!' she exclaimed. 'I wasn't asking for a definition. I know perfectly well what a metaphor is. And I also know perfectly well what a message is, and whether it comes from this side or the other.'

They stared at each other in startled silence. Elise herself was as shocked by her own outburst as Philip had been. She just couldn't believe she had spoken like this to Philip. And she was deeply wounded and alarmed by the evidently hostile intention behind Philip's words.

Philip broke the silence by getting up from the table, murmuring something about not being late for work.

And it was that same morning that Elise's father rang up and more or less told her that her marriage was on the rocks.

That evening, of course, there was a reconciliation. But a precedent had been set, and similar little altercations followed. They were all occasioned by Elise's unguarded references to the spiritual world. She never raised any objections to his increasingly frequent statements made from a purely materialistic point of view. She noted them with dismay, but said nothing. And she tried to be careful and not provoke him with too free a reference to her intangible world. But she grieved bitterly over the way he was evidently distancing himself more and more from it, remembering with sorrow how happy he had been to discover this set of values so different from his own. And sometimes she forgot to guard her tongue, a discipline she had never been used to.

At home she had had her mother to support her in her beliefs; and her father's scepticism had been cloaked in the form of an indulgent smile. He didn't believe any of this nonsense, but it amused and touched him that his little girl should display this refreshing candour. When, in spite of his doubts, Elise had insisted on marrying Philip, her father had felt a touch of jealousy as well as a certain disquiet as to the outcome of a marriage between two people with such a diametrically opposed way of seeing the world. He knew only too well what the difficulties would be. He never quite forgave Elise for her marriage, though he never held it against Philip. Philip, after all, was only doing what any man would do in the circumstances. It seemed perfectly obvious to him that any man in his senses would jump at the chance of marrying a girl like Elise. Just as he himself had married a girl very like Elise a generation before. In both cases he was inclined to feel that the men could hardly be blamed for the choice, whereas the women should have known better.

Elise was never quite able to stop herself from prattling on as she had always done about this unseen world she felt so at home in. And she frequently managed to annoy Philip even without the use of words. If he started to come up the stairs when she was on her way down she would turn hastily and run back up, for she knew it was unlucky to cross someone on the stairs. If Philip came in on a wet day and left an open umbrella in the house she would turn pale with apprehension and cross her fingers in an attempt to placate the evil spirits summoned by this unholy object.

'You and your barbaric beliefs!' he said to her one day. 'Can't you see what a fear-ridden world you've made for yourself?'

'I haven't made it.'

'Who made it then? Your God? Why does he surround you with all these traps and terrors? He's supposed to be a God of love, isn't he?'

'He *is* a God of love. And all you have to do to avoid the traps and terrors is obey the rules.'

'Rules? What rules? Where did you get them? Who gave them to you?'

'Our ancestors.'

'Yours, not mine.'

'What about the laws of physics? Where did you get them?'

'They were discovered, by scientists. People like Aristotle and Galileo and Newton and . . . '

'Ancestors,' she pointed out. 'Ancestors, every one of them. I don't see why the one set should be any more reliable than the other.'

'Simply because what my lot says is verifiable.'

'So is what my lot says.'

'How? And by whom?'

'By people. It's a matter of human experience. And who verifies your experiments?'

'Scientists. Trained scientists.'

'Not people?' she asked innocently.

Philip stared at her with what he had to admit to himself was something rather near to hate. It's not fair, he thought, she doesn't play the game. There seems to be no way of getting her to stick to one set of rules. She keeps shifting from one ground to another, just as it suits her. I suppose that's the trouble with having to deal with someone who hasn't got a trained mind.

After some months of this sort of exchange their arguments became less frequent. But not because they had come to any sort of understanding. It was simply a matter of an almost total loss of communication. Philip spent more of his free time at work – always some new experiment or other that needed a bit of extra time, it appeared. When he was at home he tended to seek shelter behind the covers of a book. And it was never the sort of book he could possibly discuss with Elise.

And Elise mourned the loss of her husband's love, and could think of no way of winning it back. If he insisted that the only form of communication was to be a purely rational and intellectual one, then there was nothing she could do.

She toyed with the idea of trying to learn something about physics so as to be able to converse with him – but how could she ever learn enough to meet him on his own level? Even if such a thing had been possible, she realized that it would have made no difference. What she needed to do was to change her way of seeing the world. And she knew that this she could never do. It wasn't a matter of loyalty to her old ways. It was simply a matter of what you see or what you don't see. You can't stop seeing something that's there simply because seeing it leads to problems with the partially blind.

By the time that Clive and Myra were blissfully expecting their first child, Elise was in a state of obvious depression. Clive had a word with Philip, but was unable to persuade him to do anything about it.

'Look, Clive, there's not a thing I can do. Nothing any rational person can do. She's away with the fairies. The only person who can really talk to her is her mother, for the simple reason that she's just as bad.'

When Clive told his wife about this conversation they decided that Myra must have a talk with Elise and see what could be done.

Myra found her looking sad and absent, and tackled her on the subject. In the end Elise agreed that she would be better to get out and about a bit more, and accepted Myra's invitation to go with her to the private viewing of an exhibition of paintings by a friend of one of Clive's brothers.

When the appointed day came Elise was reluctant to go, but felt she could hardly go back on her promise. She knew she wouldn't enjoy being in a crowd of strangers, most of them probably talking clever artistic talk which she knew she wouldn't even be able to begin to understand. She took comfort in the thought that Myra would be equally out of it, and hoped they would be able to keep each other in countenance.

'Who is the artist, anyway?' she asked as they drove there.

'A Spaniard who lives in the South of France and who comes over here every so often to exhibit. I met him once and he's very nice, but I've never seen any of his paintings. Just hope they won't all be too abstract.'

'Me too,' said Elise fervently.

Their hope was fulfilled. The paintings were all recognizable as landscapes, painted in warm, glowing colours. What Elise liked most was the effect of light in them all – a slanting, radiant light that gave an almost other-worldly touch to the canvases. The trees, the fields, the hills and the houses were all solid, three-dimensional, very much of the earth, earthy. But this almost ethereal light lifted the whole thing out of the purely material and representational. Elise at once recognized a spiritual element that made her feel at home. She forgot all about the other people, the clever talk she had so feared. She even forgot about Myra, and wandered about from one painting to another, lost and liberated.

She was standing in front of one of the smaller paintings, representing a field with a few olive trees, and with a small hut in the background. A loosely sketched figure of a man, with a hoe over his shoulder, was walking towards the hut. The colours were more sombre than in most of the other paintings, with a hint of approaching darkness. The rays of the setting sun seemed to be guiding the man back to his house. The title was 'Homecoming'.

Elise stood in front of this picture, and realized that the tears were brimming in her eyes. She felt as if she had been in exile for a long, long time, and had at last come home.

After a while she blinked the tears away and was just moving on to look at another picture when Myra appeared.

'Ah, there you are! I've been looking for you. I'd like you to meet Miquel Planas. My friend, Elise Locke.'

Elise found herself shaking hands with a small, dark man who looked about forty years old.

'Are you the artist?' she asked, wondering whether his English was good enough to carry on a conversation. He looked distinctly foreign, with his swarthy colouring and dark, bright eyes.

It turned out that Miquel Planas spoke perfect English. He explained that he had been brought over to London as a child during the Spanish Civil War, and had grown up in England. He admitted that he missed his native Catalonia terribly, but had sworn he would never go back to live there under Franco. 'So I live in the South of France most of the time, as that is the nearest I can get to Spain. And I come back here, to my second home, at regular intervals.'

He was soon surrounded by a crowd of admirers, and Elise drifted away, regretfully. She would have liked to be able to talk to him about his paintings, and what they represented for him. They had made such an impact on her that she felt she needed to discuss them with their creator.

'Do you like them?' she asked Myra, as they drove back afterwards.

'Yes, I do. I think they're very attractive. And you?'

'I can't tell you what I think of them. I honestly don't know. I just can't find words for it. I don't think I've ever seen anything I . . . I needed so much. I think they've restored my vision. I feel as if I'd been blind for months and months – years, perhaps.'

When they parted outside Elise's house Myra was disconcerted to see the tears in her friend's eyes as she thanked her. She drove home reflecting on Elise's greater artistic sensitivity. I just thought they were attractive, she reflected, and yet Elise seems to have seen so much in them that I missed. For her they seem to have been . . . well, a sort of healing. I'm so glad I took her.

Elise hardly slept that night. She kept thinking of the pictures. But she had seen too many, too quickly, to have a clear recollection of any of them except the little one with the olive trees and the homeward-bound figure. She would have liked to be able to tell Philip about them. She had made an attempt that evening.

'Myra took me to see that exhibition I was telling you about,' she volunteered.

'Oh yes? What was it like?'

'It was . . . oh, I don't know. Extraordinary.'

'One of those!' And he picked up his book.

By morning she had decided she must go back. She would have liked to speak to the artist again, but the main thing was to see the pictures, and get a clear idea of at least some of them in her head. She closed the door on her way out, then opened it again and went back into the house. A moment later she came out again. This time her chequebook lay in her bag. She walked down the path almost defiantly.

The gallery was quiet when she got there, with just a few people drifting through, looking at the pictures. She made straight for the one called 'Homecoming'. She noticed that quite a few of the pictures now had little red dots stuck to them, and it suddenly struck her that perhaps this picture had been sold too. She was relieved to see that it had no red dot attached to it, and settled down to another examination of the little scene.

She became aware of people standing behind her, talking, and realized that they were discussing this very painting.

'Yes . . . yes . . . I do like it, very much. One of the best, I'd say.'

'And it's only two hundred.'

Elise took to her heels and almost ran to the table in the entrance hall.

'I want to buy one of the pictures, please. The one called "Homecoming". I didn't notice the number.'

'That's all right. Number twenty-seven. How do you wish to pay?'

Elise already had her chequebook out. She could hardly believe she was writing out a cheque for two hundred pounds for a picture Philip hadn't even seen, and probably wouldn't like anyway. But her sense of relief at having got there in time was so great that nothing else seemed to matter.

As she walked back to have another look at the picture that was now hers she met the couple who had been admiring it on their way to the table. She hoped they weren't going to be too disappointed. If only she could explain to them how much she needed this picture, and make them understand! It wasn't a case of selfishness, it was a matter of sheer survival.

She spent a long time examining all the pictures, frequently going back to have another look at hers. She knew she would have to wait a few weeks before getting it, till the exhibition was over, but that didn't worry her. She could always come back and look at it in the meantime, whenever she felt like it.

As she was about to leave the building she met Miquel Planas coming in. He recognized her at once and came and spoke to her. She was telling him how much she liked his work when he interrupted her with the words, 'Why are you so sad?'

'But I'm not sad! I'm really very happy. I've just bought one of your paintings.'

'I am glad to know you've bought one of my paintings. But you are very sad, all the same.'

'How do you know?'

'I look at people. All the time I am looking at people. And some are opaque – you just can't see through them. But your light is clear, it tells no lies. And I can see that deep down you are very sad.'

Elise nodded, then turned away and almost ran out of the building, afraid to stay. For she had felt an almost overwhelming temptation to fling herself into the man's arms and burst out crying like a child.

All the way home she was trying to justify this sudden, almost irresistible impulse. She came to the conclusion that it stemmed from her relief at finding some corroboration in the outside world of this certainty of hers about the existence of a world beyond the material, everyday world. After all, she had really been very deprived of support since Philip had withdrawn his allegiance. Clive and Myra were darlings, but they were every bit as rationalist and materialistic as Philip.

And then there was her father too.

The only person in her present world who seemed to share her view was her mother. And Elise was reluctant to say much on the subject to her, for fear of betraying her own unhappiness and sense of isolation. All her life she had been aware of her mother's unhappiness, and had felt that it was her job to try to mitigate this rather than add to it. This man, whom she hardly knew, seemed to be the only person proclaiming the gospel of truth, her truth. She had recognized her own type of vision in his painting, and his words had added to her conviction that here was one of her people; a fellow believer. And that, she told herself, must be why I nearly flung myself into his arms. I wonder how he would have reacted?

She was roused from her speculation by a sudden awareness of a lot of noise going on round about her, and realized that it came from the horns of the angry motorists behind her. The lights had turned green, but she had been too absorbed in her own thoughts to notice. She chided herself for her lack of attention. Feeling ashamed and guilty she sent the car shooting forward, wondering whether she was really fit to drive. After all, what if it had been the other way round? What if the lights had turned red and she hadn't even noticed? It was going to be bad enough explaining about the picture to Philip, without having to confess that she'd crashed the car as well.

She had intended to go back and visit her picture occasionally while the exhibition was on, but didn't dare go near the place in case she met Miquel again. The fact that she wanted to speak to him more than to any other human being she knew made it even more desirable to avoid him. Instead she phoned the gallery and made arrangements for the picture to be sent to her when the exhibition was over.

Every day she told herself that she must break the news to Philip. But relations between them continued as strained as ever, and she never found quite enough courage to say anything about it.

The day the picture arrived was a day of unforgettable tension. On the one hand there was the joy of seeing the picture, of feeling that she was renewing her acquaintance with it, and with its author; at the same time there was the knowledge that this was the day of the showdown – unless, of course she hid the thing away. She was so scared at the prospect of Philip's reaction that she had almost decided to do this.

And then she remembered that sooner or later the bank statement for their joint account would come in, and he would of course query the two-hundred-pounds entry. They only had this one account from which all expenses incurred by either were paid, and whenever the statement came in they went over it together, discussing all major items.

So far this had seemed a perfectly reasonable thing to do, and it had never occurred to her that a time might come when she would have liked a little more financial independence.

She was standing beside the fireplace in the sitting room when Philip came in. The picture was resting on the mantelpiece, where he could hardly fail to see it right away.

He saw it, and stopped in his tracks. 'Where did you get that?'

'I bought it at that exhibition Myra took me to. Do you like it?'

'Hmn! It's all right, I suppose. I didn't think we really needed another picture.'

I needed this one, thought Elise. But she didn't dare put her conviction into words.

After looking at the picture in silence for a moment Philip asked, 'How much?'

'Two hundred.' The words came in little more than a whisper.

'Two hundred *pounds*?'

Elise nodded.

'Two hundred pounds for a *picture*? Two hundred pounds for that? And it isn't even properly drawn. Just look at that figure! Sketched in just anyhow. That's not proper drawing, that could be anyone.'

'Yes, that could be anyone. You or me. Just someone going home.'

There was a long silence, broken at last by Philip.

'Going home, you said. Is that what you want to do?'

'More than anything else in this world.'

'Back to your mother, you mean?'

'No. Back to you.'

'But you are with me.'

'How much?'

Philip looked at her defensively. 'As much as my work schedule permits.'

'That's not what I meant.'

Philip considered her answer for a moment, then allowed his anger to take the place of any serious examination of the issue.

'I just can't understand what's got into you. First of all you choose a picture for the house without consulting me. Up till now everything, but everything, we've got for the house we have chosen together, after due consultation. Secondly, you embark gaily on a major item of expenditure for something totally unnecessary. And thirdly . . . By the way, when did you buy it?'

'The day after the exhibition opened.'

'That is, weeks ago?'

Elise nodded.

'And thirdly,' Philip repeated, making sure that none of the force of his three-pronged attack was lost, 'you keep the whole matter from me all this time. I begin to see what you mean when you suggest that we aren't all that much together. I would never have expected this sort of underhand dealing from you, Elise. I don't know what I've done to deserve it.'

And that was the end of the conversation, and of all conversation, for the evening.

Elise was too depressed to go to bed at the usual time, and sat up till long after Philip had gone upstairs. When she went up she found the bedroom empty. She looked along the landing and saw light coming from under the door of the spare bedroom. Just then, as if to make matters absolutely clear, she heard a faint click, and the shaft of light disappeared.

When Philip got up the next morning Elise had gone, and so had the painting. She had left a note saying, 'I'm going home.'

He was too angry to do anything about it at first. If she'd rather be back home with Mummy, then she can jolly well stay there, he kept telling himself. But after two days he could no longer stand the misery and loneliness, and rang up her parents' house. Elise wasn't there, and neither of her parents had the slightest idea of where she could be. Suddenly the words of her note seemed to point to a sinister possibility.

5

For the third time Natana was climbing the stairs leading up to Philip's flat. It had been a great relief to her, on the previous occasion, that there had been no reply. As she had rung the bell she had felt distinctly breathless. It's the stairs, she had told herself. I've been going too fast. But she knew she hadn't been going at all fast. As she wrote her note, giving herself at least a week's grace, she decided she must take herself in hand and not get into such a state of apprehension next time.

And she had taken herself in hand, with a solid programme of meditation, long walks, and frequent reference to her mother's book. The latter exercise was, along with the walks and meditation, intended to help her overcome her nervousness; but its purpose was also to enable her to meet the objections that she had every reason to expect from Philip. And this was what she felt so nervous about. The success of her enterprise depended entirely on her being able to overcome his almost certain hostility to the book. Natana shared her mother's beliefs, and was prepared to defend them in all ordinary circumstances. But this business of proselytizing was quite new to her. Still, it was a call, she felt, and was determined to do her best to comply.

This time she paused before ringing, just to make sure she wasn't out of breath. No, she decided, she was breathing perfectly normally. That proves I'm not nervous, she told herself, and rang. In spite of this comforting assertion she felt a sudden almost ungovernable desire to turn and run as soon as she heard the footsteps approaching on the other side of the door.

Philip had filled in the time with a careful study of the book, and had found it a very frustrating experience. He had to admit that it was well written and well reasoned, and this admission continued to go against his principles, as it had on his initial reading of the first chapter. The only fault he could find with it was simply the fact that he disagreed violently with all its basic assumptions. He was looking forward to meeting Natana so as to be able to put forward his point of view, explain the total lack of any basis in reality to be found in the book's assertions, and thus demolish the whole structure. He was also looking forward to having some of the mysteries solved – who was Natana, who was Savamindra, what was the connexion? Were they the same person? And why was this girl so anxious for him to read the book? Yes, he was looking forward to meeting Natana.

So much so that, when he heard the bell ringing that Monday evening and realised this might be her promised visit, he paused and took a deep breath before opening the door. He was feeling quite breathless.

He found himself looking at a small, dark, extremely pretty girl. Very young, obviously much too young to have written such a book. She was looking at him out of dark, round, glowing eyes. Her lips were parted, as if she were about to say something, but no words came. Philip had no difficulty in finding the right words.

'You're Natana,' he announced.

The girl nodded.

He led her into the sitting room and they sat down, facing each other across the slanting rays of evening sunshine. She really was remarkably pretty, he decided, as he looked at the short, dark hair, thick and straight and vigorous, that framed the lively young face, with its olive skin and strong, expressive features. The lips were full and very red, the nose slightly aquiline, the chin rounded and determined. Altogether a young woman to be reckoned with as well as admired, he decided, and wondered whether there was perhaps a trace of Jewish blood in her ancestry.

They examined each other in silence for a moment.

Natana at least had known, more or less, what to expect, having seen a photograph of Philip in his youth. She decided that she would certainly have recognized him, in spite of the changes which the years had brought. But twenty years does make a difference, she thought. More than my whole lifetime! Still, he's not bad for his age. He's kept his hair and his figure, and certainly looks more interesting than he did as a young man. But there's just something about him . . . a little bit pedantic, a little bit old-maidish.

Then she chided herself for coming to any such conclusion, or any conclusion at all, when she had only just met him and hardly even heard him pronounce half a dozen words. I'm prejudiced, she thought, that's what it is. And I mustn't allow myself to be prejudiced. It's the last thing Mummy would have wanted.

'I'm sorry I wasn't in when you called last week,' he said. There were so many questions to be asked that he didn't know where to start, so a commonplace formula seemed to provide as good a starting point as anything else. They could go on gently from that to the more important issues.

But Natana wasn't prepared to take things gently. 'I wasn't sorry,' she stated. 'In fact, I was quite relieved,' she confessed with disarming frankness.

'Oh! In that case, I might as well admit that I too was more than a little relieved.'

'Why?'

'Because I hadn't finished reading the book. And why were you relieved to find that I wasn't at home?'

Natana hesitated. 'I'm afraid you're going to think me very rude. There are a number of things that you're bound to want to know, including this one, that I'd rather not explain just yet. I will tell you them, honest, I promise I'll answer every question you ask, but not at once, not always just when you want to know the answer. I know that sounds odd, and rather arbitrary, but I promise you I have a very good reason for what I'm asking. So do you mind if . . . if we stick to my rules, for the time being?'

Philip laughed, delighted. With the promise of ultimate elucidation he could happily accept this new element of mystery.

'My dear young lady,' he said in his most avuncular tone, 'I'm perfectly willing to play the game according to your rules. Especially since you've promised to explain all in the long run.'

'That's very kind of you. I know it must sound odd and rather dictatorial, and I know you're the kind of man who likes to know things, so this must make it difficult for you.'

'How do you know what kind of a man I am?'

'Later, if you don't mind. That's one of the things that has to wait, I'm afraid.'

'And explaining why you can't tell me now is presumably also one of the things that has to wait?'

She nodded, and Philip nodded too. 'Self-evident, that one, wasn't it? So I'd better leave it to you to regulate the conversation. But just one more question, if I may. Where did you get this wonderful name, Natana?'

'That one I think we can cope with right away. Have you ever heard of the mediaeval Catalan writer Ramon Llull?'

'No, never.'

'Well, before I was born my mother was reading his most famous book, *Blanquerna* – or rather, my father, who was a Catalan, was reading it and translating it for her, and she liked the book and the name of one of the principal characters so much that she decided that she would call me after her, if I was a girl. And I was.'

'And so you are Natana. It's a wonderful name. And now it's up to you. You can tell me or ask me what you wish. I have no regulations to lay down.'

Natana smiled. 'Just as well. They might prove incompatible with mine if you had, and we'd never get started.'

Philip wondered precisely what it was they were to get started on. Not that he would have minded, really, whatever it was. Any sort of a conversation with this original and attractive personality would be welcome.

Natana settled herself in her armchair, took a deep breath, and said, 'What I really came for was to know what you thought of the book.'

'Which is just what I expected, though I still haven't got the slightest idea of why you left it here in the first place.'

'If that's a concealed question I shall just have to ignore it. Can you tell me what you think of the book?'

'I . . . I thought it was extremely well written. The style was very pleasing, the book was well organised, well argued. But . . . ' he added, seeing Natana's eyes lighting up with pleasure and surprise, ' . . . but, I have to say that I simply couldn't agree with any of the premises on which the arguments are founded.'

'Which means that you accept none of the conclusions?'

'Exactly.' He was sorry to see the disappointment in Natana's face. It was a pity, but there was nothing he could do about that. He wasn't going to lie to the girl. 'Anyway,' he added, 'that doesn't mean there's nothing more to be said about the book. I was certainly surprised by the wide range that the author attributes to the idea of the occult. Meditation, mysticism, the psychology of the unconscious . . . '

'You thought it would be nothing but Tarot cards and a lady with a turban gazing into a crystal ball?'

Philip laughed. 'Sort of. I suppose that was rather naive of me.'

'I would say prejudiced and ignorant, rather than naive.'

'Then *I* suggest that it's you who are being naive in assuming you can come in here and call me prejudiced and ignorant, and still hope to have any sort of reasonable discussion.'

They gazed at each other in mutual hostility. Then Natana leaned forward in her chair, as if to bridge the gap between them, and said, 'I'm sorry. That was rude of me. It's just that I should have thought that you, as a physicist, might have been accessible to some of the reasoning.'

'As a physicist? We're all scientists too, you know, in the world of physics. We don't deal with the unfalsifiable.'

'Yes, I know. But some of the developments in physics over the last fifty years or so . . . well, they seem to suggest that there is more than one way of looking at things, that the answer is different depending on how you pose the question. I think it's called the principle of complementarity, isn't it?'

'How on earth do you know about the principle of complementarity? Have you studied physics? You look much too young to have studied anything.'

Natana bridled. 'I'm nearly twenty. But no, I haven't studied physics. However, my mother went into all this very carefully.'

'Your mother? Did your mother write the book?'

'Yes. I didn't mean to tell you just yet, but I don't suppose it matters. Yes, she wrote the book and I helped her – oh, just with typing and the index and things like that.'

'So, you're Savamindra's daughter? That, I presume, was a nom de plume?'

'Yes. It just came to her one day.'

'In a burst of inspiration?'

'You can laugh if you like. She had quite a laugh about it herself, but she was a very intuitive woman all the same.'

'Was?'

'She died last year. Just after the book came out. I was so thankful she lived to see it in print. Anyway, I had hoped that if we discussed the book we might find some common ground. But it seems you don't admit that the whole theory of relativity, the principle of complementarity, etc, which are mentioned in the book – you don't feel all that opens the way to an acceptance of some non-rational type of truth?'

'My dear Natana, you can't expect a man who has spent the last thirty years in the service of physics to discuss the matter with someone who simply hasn't studied it at all. We just don't have enough vocabulary in common.'

While waiting for Natana's visit Philip had been wondering how convincing he could make this line of argument sound. The girl had picked on the very aspect of the book that he felt least able to refute. If indeed there were more than one way of looking at truth, and his own discipline clearly pointed in this direction, then he realized that it was going to be very difficult to convince the unscientifically minded that this did not mean that one could accept every theory that contradicted the known laws of the universe. After all, the infidel – scientifically speaking – simply had to ask: why not accept this other apparently irrational view as well? Why not accept my spiritually oriented view of reality, if reality is manifold? In his perplexity Philip had fallen back on the slightly dishonest stratagem of dazzling the opponent with his own knowledge, and claiming that there was no common ground on which to carry on an argument. Rather to his relief, he saw Natana's discomfiture.

She had suddenly realized that she was utterly unfitted to argue with a man of Philip's calibre. How could she have thought she could get away with it?

But Natana was not easily defeated, and she was very adept at switching to a different approach on short notice. She now decided that the only way to reach Philip was through the personal and emotional. There was still hope that, once he knew the truth about the book and its origins, he might view it with less disfavour.

'Well,' she said, 'it seems there's nothing more to be said where the content of the book is concerned. As you say, the vocabulary is missing, on my side certainly, and I suspect also on yours. So I can now go ahead and answer all your questions.'

Philip wasn't any too pleased at the suggestion that their dialectical impasse might be due to his own limitations as well as to hers.

'And the first thing I must tell you, I suppose, is my reason for not answering your questions before. The thing is, you see, I was a little apprehensive about . . . about how you would react when you knew who the author of the book was.'

'Your mother? Who was your mother, then? And why should I react against her?'

'Because she was your first wife.'

There was a silence. Then Philip spoke.

'So Elise is dead?'

'Yes. And the last years of her life were dominated by her desire to write this book for you, in the hope that it would be some sort of reparation for having walked out on you.'

'Oh, God, Natana!' Philip felt immensely distressed and at the same time the cynic in him was murmuring, 'Who but Elise would think of a scheme like that? To try to make amends with the very beliefs that ruined our marriage!'

To Natana he said, 'I can't think why I never thought of that possibility. It is so very much her type of thought.' Then he had to admit to himself that for well over twenty years he had been trying to forget all about Elise, and seemed to have succeeded pretty well. 'I suppose,' he added, putting forward a more acceptable excuse, 'I suppose it was because I never thought of her as ever writing anything. Especially such an almost scholarly type of book. For it is a remarkably serious piece of work.'

'I think my father must take some of the credit for that. He had written quite a few books about the philosophy of art, so he knew how to set about it. She had told him she wanted to write it, and he encouraged her and helped her enormously in the early stages.'

'And then? What about the later stages?'

'He died five years ago, when the book was only in its infancy. And that's why it became a sort of double duty to my mother to get it finished. For you and for him.'

'And after she died you took up the torch and have set out to complete the task?'

'To try to.'

They sat in silence for a while. Then Philip said, 'Look, Natana, all this has come as a great shock to me, as you can imagine. We'll talk more about the book and the ideas expressed in it. But not today. I can't cope with it today.'

Natana made as if to stand up.

'No, don't go yet. There are a lot of things I want to know. I thought I had quite a few questions to ask in the first place, but now there are many more.'

'And more important ones, I suppose.'

'Now I see how it was that you knew what sort of a person I am. And it was a good idea to try to get me to read and discuss the book without knowing who the author was, just in case I was prejudiced. Which I may well be.'

Natana was looking at him with a little smile playing about her lips. 'There was another reason too. It struck me that, if I handed the book in and said nothing about it, well, you might be intrigued by the touch of mystery, and pay more attention.'

Philip thought of the way the unexplained arrival of the book had almost obsessed him, and nodded thoughtfully. 'Yes, it was a pretty good ploy. What with that, and your noncommittal little note last week, you certainly succeeded in arousing my curiosity. You get full marks for strategy. But tell me more about your mother. After the divorce came through I knew she had married this Spanish artist, and that was the last I heard. If I'd known he was a Catalan I might have seen the connexion when you told me you'd got your name from a Catalan writer. Tell me, what did she die of?'

'A cerebral haemorrhage. She suddenly turned ill one morning, and in a few hours she was dead.'

'That must have been a terrible shock to you.'

'Yes. No warning, neither of us had any warning.'

Philip was reminded of the conversation with Elise all those years ago, when she had told him of the message her friend's mother had received about her own imminent death. It's a pity, he thought cynically, that the spirit world isn't a bit more systematic about this sort of thing. A word of warning might have spared this poor girl a terrible shock.

'And this was last year?'

'Yes, just over six months ago. I can hardly believe it yet.'

'And your father died five years ago, you said? Was that sudden too?'

'No. He died of cancer and we'd all known for a long time he was going to die. It's easier that way.'

'For you perhaps. But surely not for him?'

'It was for him I meant. It might not be for some people, but when you're the kind of man my father was, that's the best way.'

Philip felt completely out of his depths. Here was this girl, not yet twenty, able to accept the death of both her parents and talk about it serenely and in a simple, matter-of-fact way.

It must have something to do with her beliefs, he thought. Faced with the sudden news of Elise's death, and with the knowledge that she had been thinking of him during her last years, he felt shaken and at a loss. The girl's comforting beliefs, he knew, were utterly unfounded, and he couldn't imagine himself ever being able to share them. But he had to admit they seemed to serve some useful purpose for all that.

'One last question, for today at any rate,' he said after a pause. 'How did you know my address?'

'Mummy kept in touch with her old friend Julia Bowen, your friend Clive's sister. She told her about all the changes of address, your second marriage and the end of your second marriage, and . . . and everything,' she ended up rather lamely.

'And that, in fact, is just about everything. There have been no other major changes in my life.' He smiled rather grimly. It didn't sound like a very successful record.

'I suppose I'd better go now,' she said, remembering he had announced that the previous question was to be the last one. 'Can I come back?'

'Please, please do come back. There are still so many things I want to ask you. And we still have to talk about the book. Only I can't cope with anything else just now.'

'I know. It must all have been quite a shock. I'm sorry if I mismanaged it. Perhaps I could have told you it all more tactfully.'

'No, you were perfect. You have nothing to reproach yourself with. Can you come back tomorrow?'

'I'd love to. Same time?'

'Come earlier. Come and have a meal. I'm not much of a cook, but . . . '

'Ah, but I am! I'll help you. I love other people's kitchens.'

Philip smiled at her, amused and touched by the girl's self-confidence and enthusiasm. He was suddenly reminded of Elise, the Elise who walked about carrying a rose and making statements about the importance of beauty. And he found himself wondering what had happened to all the trust and enthusiasm of the young Elise. Her joy and confidence had faded and withered, along with the rose and all its delicate beauty. And he thought of Blake's poem, 'O Rose, thou art sick!' Was it his love that had destroyed Elise? It hadn't been dark and secret, but it seemed to have had as deadly an effect.

After the girl had gone he went and sat down again in the same place, gazing at the now empty chair Natana had occupied, and reliving his early years with Elise. He sat there till long after it was dark, gazing into the chair, which was lit up by the light from the street lamp, as if to emphasize its emptiness. And the missing form that should have been sitting in the chair was not that of Natana, but her mother's. He felt stunned and sad, with the hopeless, despairing sadness of an old, long-dead, long-forgotten love, when death has stepped in and made it clear that now, as never before, there is absolutely nothing to hope for. All the old love and all the old happiness have gone for ever and for ever. And the early years come back with an obsessive insistence, and you feel that nothing will ever again be as fresh and true and powerful as that old, long-dead love. And even the moments of anger and torment have gone beyond recall, and this too is an unbearable grief. And everything else – your present life, the years in between – everything is swallowed up in the anguish of the irrecoverable.

He slept little that night, and felt so oppressed the following morning that he decided he'd take a day off, and phoned his secretary to say he wouldn't be in. Then he thought of all the hours that still separated him from Natana's visit, and felt he would have been better to go to work after all. That would at least have helped to pass the time. But he was committed now. Instead he drove out into the country and had a long walk over the downs.

By the time he got back, the worst of his depression had lifted. He was anxious to see Natana again. There were so many things he had to ask her. If Elise really had written the book for him, to make reparation for leaving him, then it appeared that she must have held herself at least partly to blame. In a way this made things worse. For, however hard he had protested to himself that he was in no way to blame for the breakup of the marriage, he realized now that his determination to put the whole thing out of his consciousness stemmed from a hidden feeling of guilt. And if Elise had been able to face her own guilt in the matter and try to make some sort of amends, that certainly put her well ahead of him in the moral stakes. Philip didn't very much like having anyone ahead of him, no matter what the context.

As the time of Natana's visit approached, Philip found himself thinking more and more of the last few months of his life with Elise. He had been intensely unhappy, he had been aware of the fact that she was unhappy too, but he had no sense of the impending disaster. He tried to remember the details of their conversation on the subject of the painting, but all he could remember clearly was that he had objected to the sketchy drawing of the figure. And the fact that it had been called 'Homecoming'. And this reminded him of the misunderstanding about where she had gone. To her mother, of course, had seemed the obvious interpretation of the words in her note. *I'm going home*, she had written. How was he to know he was supposed to take that metaphorically?

As he waited for the daughter to arrive he sat in a kind of trance, trying after all those years to relive what the mother must have felt as she walked out of her home for the last time, abandoning her husband and her whole way of life, taking with her nothing but a few clothes and the picture that had acted as the catalyst in this dramatic change in both their lives.

6

It was five o'clock in the morning when Elise crept down the stairs, carrying a small suitcase in one hand and a carrier bag containing the picture in the other. She closed the front door behind her with infinite caution, afraid she might waken Philip. The bedroom he had chosen to sleep in was immediately above.

As she stepped on to the gravel of the path she heard a slight crunch, and moved over to the flower-bed instead. Stepping carefully, to avoid hurting any of the flowers, she got as far as the gate and out on to the pavement. Her anxiety made her tread softly for at least the first hundred yards. Not, of course, that Philip could really have done anything to stop her, had he known of her departure – assuming he wanted to stop her anyway. But she just couldn't face the thought of a confrontation. She didn't see how she could ever bear to speak to him again, after what she could only view as the ultimate act of hostility and rejection, his decision to sleep alone, without even telling her of his intention. No, Philip had written her off completely, and there was nothing for it but to go away and leave him in his bare, two-dimensional, measurable world.

The familiar landscape looked oddly unfamiliar at this early hour. It was already daylight, but the street-lighting was still on, shining bleakly at intervals along the road. There was no traffic about, and she found the silence unnerving. And not a single living being was to be seen. The whole suburb looked as if all its inhabitants had fallen into a long, oblivious sleep, from which there was nothing to waken them. With blinds and curtains drawn, the houses turned inscrutable faces towards her, keeping her out almost wilfully, making her feel doubly rejected.

She at last got to the underground station, and had to wait a long time for a train. Then another long wait before the train for Victoria arrived. Another wait in Victoria Station for the train to Dover. It was mid morning before she got there, as there had been a slight accident with a goods train earlier on, and the line wasn't yet clear.

At Dover she learned that the boat she was to take hadn't arrived so far – there was some sort of dispute going on at the Calais end, and no one really knew when it would be in. She'd better join the queue, all the same, or she might not get on to the first boat. It took nearly two hours for the boat to arrive and take on its new complement of passengers. By that time the queue had grown to immense proportions, and Elise spent the whole journey jammed into a corner between a pile of luggage and one of the lifeboats, with other distressed passengers vomiting beside her.

Things didn't improve for some time even after they got to Calais. The industrial dispute was still causing delays, and it took at least another hour for her to be able to get off the boat. After that things became less exhausting. She got a seat in the Paris train, and hoped she'd be able to sleep during the journey. But the rest of the compartment was occupied by a cheerfully argumentative family of French peasants. Her school French was utterly defeated by their patois, and she never managed to make out what they were arguing about. What she had no doubts about was the family's addiction to garlic. The smell seemed to ooze from their very pores. Elise quite liked the smell of garlic, but not second-hand. She tried taking refuge in the corridor, but discovered it was a choice of evils, for the toilets emitted a strong smell of stale urine. The combination of the smells, the noise, her exhaustion, her moral anguish and her apprehension, was almost more than she could bear.

In Paris she found that there would be a train leaving for Perpignan at ten o'clock. That gave her about five hours with nothing to do but change stations and buy her ticket – a terrifying programme for her, as she had never had to do anything like this on her own before. She thought with sadness of the fact that before her marriage she would have considered this an exciting challenge. But Philip had done everything of the sort for her – at first out of his desire to cherish her, and later out of his conviction of her total incompetence in the material world. The result had been a great loss of confidence on her part.

Had she not been so exhausted when she at last lay down on her couchette she might have derived some satisfaction from the fact that she had coped with her difficult assignment. All she had to do now was leave the train at Perpignan and get a taxi to take her to the address she had already memorised – just in case, through some weird mischance, she should lose the catalogue she had been given at the preview of Miquel Planas' paintings.

She had determined that she was not going to think about anything beyond that point. But as she lay on her narrow bunk thoughts of the reception that might await her kept coming, filling her with the deepest misgiving, making her wonder at her own temerity. After all, she knew nothing about the man; really nothing at all. Was he married? She didn't even know that. And if so, might her arrival there not cause immense problems? What wife was going to believe that a woman who was virtually a perfect stranger would suddenly turn up unannounced, expecting refuge?

Would Miquel be able to convince an unprepared wife that there had been nothing whatever between them to warrant this sudden visitation? And anyway, even if there was no wife – or lover, for that matter – to take into consideration, what would Miquel himself think? How could she explain her action to him – how could she explain it to herself?

The nearer she got to her destination the more unaccountable and inexcusable the whole thing seemed. She had no doubts about her rightness in leaving Philip. That was the only thing she could do; she had no choice. It was Philip who had rejected her. But how could she justify her running to a perfect stranger for help?

And then she thought of the paintings, of her painting, lying on the rack above her, and of the conviction she had felt that this man knew, that he belonged to her world, that he had recognised her as one of his people. The proof was the fact that not only had he seen her sadness, but had spoken of it. He'll understand, she thought, and fell into an uneasy sleep.

She woke up, suddenly aware of the fact that the train had stopped, and realised she must have slept for several hours, as it was now broad daylight. Peering out of the window she could just see the end of a board with half a word written on it. '—ignan,' it said. She leapt down to the floor, grabbed her possessions, and jumped off the train as it was beginning to gather speed. Only then did she manage to see the complete word – Perpignan. She heaved a sigh of relief. For all she knew there might have been another station with a name ending in '—ignan,' and she might have been many miles from her destination.

The station seemed deserted. If there had been any passengers getting off the same train they had had enough time to get away by now. As far as she could see, she had the place to herself. She looked at her watch, which told her it was just after six. Must have stopped, she thought. It can't be that early. Then she found a clock in the waiting room. Three minutes past six. She had been told in Paris that the journey took all night, and had forgotten to ask when exactly the train reached Perpignan. Six in the morning seemed inconsiderately early, and apparently the station staff thought so too, for not one of them was to be seen. Not feeling very hopeful, she walked out of the main entrance in search of a taxi.

From where she stood she could see that the station seemed to be on the outskirts of the town. There was a straggling street facing her, from which another took off at right angles, looking as if it led to the centre. In the distance she could see the ground sloping up to a hill, with some buildings on it. In front of her there were one or two cafés, but she thought they must be closed at this time of the morning.

And no sign of a taxi.

She went and sat down in the waiting room. After a while she heard some voices coming from outside, and looked out. There were signs of activity in one of the cafés. Carrying her case and her bag she crossed the street and sat down at one of the tables on the pavement. The sun was already quite strong, the air warm and pleasant. If a waiter came, she decided, she would have a coffee. If not, she might as well sit here till a taxi appeared. After all, she was in no hurry. She could hardly turn up before seven in the morning!

Eventually a waiter came, stood over her and said:

'*Madame?*'

She ordered a coffee and a croissant, and was trying to enjoy the latter delicacy, in spite of her misery and apprehension, when a good-looking middle-aged man came and asked if he might share her table. As all the other tables were totally unoccupied she assumed this was meant as an advance, but could think of no polite way to tell the man not to bother. While she struggled mentally with her inadequate French the man evidently took her silence to mean consent, and sat down in the chair next to her.

Well, she thought, since he's here, I might as well find out about taxis from him. He was most helpful, most friendly, and assured her that when they had finished their respective coffees he would make all the necessary arrangements for her. She assumed that this meant calling a taxi. After a while he got up, bowed, and said, '*Je reviens, tout de suite.*' A minute later an elegant car drew up beside her table, and the man jumped out and picked up her case.

'*Mais je veux un taxi!*' she exclaimed.

The man shook his head, smiling. '*Pas de taxis à cette heure du matin, madame*,' he explained.

Elise simply didn't know whether to believe him or not. She hesitated. Her French was too poor and her spirits too low for her to embark on an argument. And the man was standing beside his car, holding the door open for her. She gave in, and sank back into the luxurious seat with a feeling of fatalistic acquiescence.

As they drove towards the centre of the town he pointed out some of the landmarks and Elise wondered whether she would soon be familiar with them.

'*Vous êtes célibataire?*' the man suddenly asked her. She hesitated, not sure of the meaning of the word. Once again he seemed to interpret her silence favourably. At the very moment that the word 'celibate' flashed into her mind, informing her that she should have answered in the negative, she saw the man give her a quick, exultant look, and realised that he had assumed her reluctance to answer indicated a willingness on her part to act as a free agent.

The man spent the rest of the journey trying to persude her to let him take her to the beach instead of the address she had given. He knew a lovely beach not far away, very quiet and secluded, '*très retirée,*' where they could spend the day.

By this time she was very worried, and wondered whether he would in fact leave her at Miquel's house, or just keep driving till they got to this quiet little plage. All she could do was keep on insisting that he was to take her to the house of '*mes amis*', hoping that the plural would make the whole thing sound more normal and everyday than it actually was. In the end he yielded. To her relief she saw the longed-for name on one of the street corners, and in a moment the car drew up and her companion got out and handed her her luggage. As she turned away after thanking him, she heard him murmur:

'*C'est dommage, quand même.*'

She just pretended to ring, in the hope that her escort would have disappeared before anyone came to the door. As soon as he had driven off she rang. All the terror of this moment, with its fear of a repudiation on Miquel's part, had been driven into the background by the more pressing worry about her escort's intentions. Now that this fear was no longer uppermost, her previous apprehension came flooding back to her, and she was trembling like a leaf by the time she heard the big, old wooden door being opened.

Miquel stood in front of her, unshaven, in his pyjamas, and she realised she had probably got him out of bed. It was, after all, not yet seven in the morning.

She stood there, shaking visibly, and saying:

'I . . . I . . . '

Miquel drew her into the house, taking her case from her.

'So you've come,' he said, without expressing any surprise.

'Were you . . . you weren't expecting me, were you?'

'Not quite. But almost.'

'I don't understand. What made you think . . . ?'

'I'll tell you later,' he said, noticing that she was on the brink of collapse. 'You must sleep first. Then we'll talk.'

He led her through a long hall with a tiled floor and supported her as she staggered up the stairs. By this time she was sobbing, and still shaking violently. They turned into a big, dimly lit room with an unmade bed in it. He left her with instructions to get into bed, and said he would come back in a few minutes.

Elise was too exhausted and distressed even to be able to open her case. She simply slipped off her dress and got into bed in her underclothes. As she lay down she noticed that the bed was warm. Five minutes ago, she thought, he was lying here. She was both shocked and comforted by the physical closeness this warmth represented.

In a few minutes Miquel came back and began opening drawers and taking things out. 'All my clothes are here,' he explained. 'I haven't got another made-up bed in the house at the moment, so it had to be this room. There,' he said, as he picked up a pair of shoes, 'I'll leave you alone now.'

'But . . . I mean, this is a . . . '

'We'll talk later, when you've slept.'

'But, please, please, there's something I must know, or I won't be able to sleep.'

'Well?'

'Are you . . . can I . . . ?'

'I'm not going to send you away. And I'm not going to force you to stay. You're a free agent. Is that what you want to know?'

Elise nodded and burst into tears.

'That's right,' he said. 'First you must cry, then you must sleep, and then we can talk.'

And with that he left the room, closing the door behind him.

Elise cried as instructed, but only for a very few minutes. After that the combination of exhaustion, misery and relief got the better of her and she fell into a deep, untroubled sleep.

An hour later Miquel heard his *femme de ménage* letting herself in and intercepted her in the hall.

'There is a lady sleeping in my bed. She is not to be disturbed, so you'll have to forget about making the bed today.'

Mme Marais nodded impassively.

'Will the lady be staying?'

'*Qui sait?*' he answered, and shrugged his shoulders.

Mme Marais shrugged hers in reply. Then she asked whether she ought to make up another bed.

'Yes, perhaps you'd better. In the room at the back.'

'*On ne sait jamais, n'est ce pas?*' remarked the lady as she picked up her basket and made her way to the kitchen.

Miquel went into the garden at the back of the house and smoked his pipe for a long time. He felt too unsettled to work. He knew he had done the right thing in insisting on sleep as the first requisite for Elise; but he had difficulty in mastering his curiosity about this not totally unexpected visit. Above all, he wanted to know what Elise would think about the fact that he had almost been expecting her. It was something he could not explain rationally, and he hoped that Elise would be able to accept an explanation based entirely on intuitive grounds.

Mme Marais, who had been in charge of his domestic arrangements for many years, was an old and trusted friend. He would have liked to give her something more in the way of an explanation of this unexpected turn of events, but this would have to wait till he himself had a clearer idea of what had happened and of how things were likely to turn out. Fortunately Mme Marais was a lady of high standards, and neither curiosity nor impatience were among her characteristics. She knew, and he realized that she knew, that in time she would be given as full a picture of the situation as he himself was ever likely to have.

After many hours Elise woke up with a very clear recollection of a dream. She was looking at an underwater scene; or rather, the scene was there, but she had no consciousness of herself, either as spectator or participator. She was simply aware of what was there; that was all. And what was there was a limited area of something that looked like the sea bed, but might have been the bottom of some huge tank, for it was a sort of oblong some ten yards long by about two or three yards deep; but she had a clear impression that there was an immeasurable depth of water above this visible fragment. And all this area was filled with stones, big flat stones piled on top of each other in a random and shifting pattern. There was some vegetation too – long, thin, reedy-looking things swaying in the water, other, smaller plants clinging to the stones. It was all resting on a bed of sand. There was very little light, and that too was constantly changing, so that at one moment a hazy light would drift into the foreground, as if carried in by the current. Then a cloud of darkness would swirl in, as if a bottle of black ink had been poured into the water. Sometimes the blackness would take on an almost granular appearance, like coal dust or even black sand, swirled round by the water. The whole picture was very sombre, but full of movement, and not frightening. And there was practically no colour, only the black changing into grey and the grey changing into black. The nearest to any colour in the whole scene was a dim, greenish tinge in the grey. Even the vegetation had this same ambiguous, muted tone.

Shortly before she awakened, a long, thin streak of brighter light appeared below one of the larger rocks. It shone for a moment, then disappeared suddenly, as if someone had switched off a light. And the watery scene continued as before, constantly changing, constantly moving, always sombre, but with different gradations of light and dark.

When she woke she still seemed to be looking into this aquatic landscape, and kept her eyes on it with the most intense interest till it faded away. She had a feeling that it was immensely significant, though she had no idea of how to interpret it.

The blinds were drawn, and the room had something of the same twilight look that had dominated her dream; but it was light enough for her to be able to see the time in her watch. It was almost seven o'clock, and she realized she must have slept for nearly twelve hours. Feeling slightly light-headed she got up and made her way downstairs, where she found Miquel sitting in the doorway of the dining-room, looking out to the high-walled garden at the back of the house.

'I had a dream,' she said. 'I don't know whether it was good or bad, but it was very vivid.'

'Can you tell me?'

She told him.

'It was a good dream,' he said, after she had finished.

'How do you know?'

'Because everything was flowing. That is how life is. That is how we should be. Flowing, ready to move with whatever life brings.'

'And that is why you have accepted my coming here without asking questions, without even letting me give an explanation?'

'Of course. What else is there to do? But I shall be

happy to hear any explanation you wish to give, now you have slept. But no, not yet. You must eat first. That too is important. Let us go and see what Mme Marais has prepared for us.'

'Who is Mme Marais?'

'She is the lady who does everything that needs to be done in this house. You will meet her tomorrow, and you are not to be afraid. She looks very severe, but she is very human. We have been friends for many years. And she is an excellent cook.'

The meal was wonderful, with a colourful array of vegetables all cooked in olive oil and flavoured with herbs.

'It looks so beautiful,' she sighed. She knew that deep down she was still intensely unhappy and uncertain. But for the moment she was able to leave all her sorrows in the background. Miquel had ordered her to eat, and she was glad to concentrate on the task in hand, in a sort of trance-like state. It struck her that perhaps this was what he meant by flowing.

After they had finished eating they cleared everything away and went and sat once again by the door, looking out into the now twilit garden.

They sat in silence for a moment, and then Miquel looked at her and laughed. 'We can talk now, you know,' he said. 'I do not intend to silence you if you wish to explain things.'

'Yes, I do, I want to. But first of all there's something I want to ask you. Why were you sort of expecting me?'

'The day I met you, I could see you were moved by my pictures. And I wanted to talk about it, but you saw what it was like, too many people about. It's always like that on the day of the opening. And then I saw you the second day, and I tried to talk to you, but you suddenly ran off. And this didn't surprise me, although at that point I hadn't yet realized that I might expect to see you here. But after you'd gone I looked to see what picture you'd bought, and when I saw what it was I began to have a suspicion that you might ultimately come home here.'

'And you were right. And I myself had not the slightest idea of anything of the kind at the time. Not till the night before I left. And it was because of your picture that we quarrelled, my husband and I.'

'But you were unhappy long before that.'

'For a long time. Our worlds had been so different, and then they converged, we lived in the same world for a year or two. And then they drifted apart. And there was nothing I could do about it.'

'Of course. There never is.'

'Never? That sounds very pessimistic.'

'Not at all. When you try to break the flow, things go wrong. When you accept it, things go right.'

'Are you saying that it was all my fault for trying to break the flow, as you put it?'

'I expect he was doing the same thing too, in his way.'

'So it was wrong of me to try to hold on to my husband?'

'Yes, quite wrong. No, don't look so shocked. Wrong not in a moral sense, we're not talking about morals. Wrong in a practical sense.'

'But if we're talking about marriage, surely we should be talking about morals?'

'What's the good of a moral code that doesn't work? You see where it got you, don't you? But tell me more about these two worlds that came together briefly – under the influence of love, I suppose. What were they like, your two worlds?'

'His was purely material and rational. And when we fell in love I thought he really had seen something of my set of values, and accepted them.'

'And your set of values? What is that?'

'It's not very rational. It's intuitive, spiritual. And when I saw your paintings I thought you belonged to that world too.'

'And now I have made you change your mind, because of my immoral statements?'

He threw his head back and roared with laughter. Elise was completely taken aback.

'Well,' she said when he had stopped laughing, 'what am I to believe?'

'Come,' he said. 'Come and I'll show you.'

He led her up two flights of stairs to a large studio at the top of the house. There were a number of paintings lying about, some finished, some hardly begun. They all had the same quality that had so impressed her at the exhibition.

'So you see,' he said, 'it's all right.'

Elise was both reassured and puzzled. 'Yes, that's what I was looking for. But I still don't understand. There seems to be a contradiction. Between *them*', she pointed to the paintings, 'and some of the things you've said. I mean, flowing's all very well, but what about commitments, what about vows?'

He was standing beside her, nodding his head. 'Yes, there is a problem. But you are in a much better position now than you were before.'

'In what way?'

'Because now you *know* there is a problem. And you know what it is.'

'So I may eventually solve it?'

'Who knows? But that's not the bit that matters. What matters is the struggle.'

'But I was struggling before.'

'Yes, but you were struggling to stay in the same place. And that's the one thing we can never manage.' He laughed again, and, as if aware that he sounded rather sententious, he added, 'Which doesn't mean, of course, that you can't stay in this one place just as long as you like. Or as long as you need, which may turn out to be much the same.'

'You mean it might be, if I learn to flow?'

The following morning when she went downstairs Miquel took her into the kitchen to meet Mme Marais, who had just arrived. Her first glimpse was of the back view of an angular figure leaning forward as she emptied a large shopping basket on to the kitchen table. Her clothes were dark and almost studiously unattractive, her hair was screwed up at the top of her head into a bun from which a number of hairpins protruded. When the woman turned round to greet the new guest she revealed a face of equally uncompromising severity. She was polite, but not forthcoming. As soon as she was alone with her host Elise said, 'I'm glad you warned me. She looks very forbidding.'

'Yes, I know. But in fact, I think there's very little that she does forbid. I'll give you a week. By then you'll be completely won over.'

'By what? What is there in her to win anyone over?'

'I don't quite know. Integrity, certainly, though that's not usually a particularly winning characteristic, and humour, of a very, very dry variety that it's easy to miss, and a great deal of realistic acceptance of things as they are.'

'You mean, she flows?'

Miquel laughed. 'Yes, I suppose that's what I do mean, though it's not what you'd expect from her appearance and manner.'

Elise's thoughts had turned from Mme Marais to what Miquel had said about giving her a week to be won over by the lady. So he expects me to stay at least that long, she thought. And she took some comfort in the statement, still feeling aghast at the thought of how precarious and provisional was her situation. This guarantee of a week's stay seemed to offer a tiny island of permanence in her suddenly unstable world.

Later that morning, when Mme Marais went upstairs to do the housework, she took note of the fact that both beds had been slept in. She nodded thoughtfully as she looked at the unmade bed in the guest's bedroom. I'll give them a week, she thought. Then we can wash this lot of sheets and put them away again.

7

For the first few days Elise could only think of her new life as of a sort of peaceful parenthesis, a chance to let her wounds begin to heal, to let her find her feet again and be able to come to some sort of a decision as to what to do with her life. When she had left London she had thought only in terms of the immediate future – she was going home, home to the sort of values she had known before her marriage.

Miquel's painting and her brief conversation with him had made it clear that here was a man with some of the spiritual insight from which she had been so cut off during the last few years. Only now, after a day or two in Miquel's house, did she begin to ask herself why she had not thought of going back to her own home, where she would have the equally appropriate company of her mother. At first she could only come up with the answer that it was her father's hostility to this way of thinking that had prevented her from taking this obvious way out of the problem of finding somewhere to go, now that Philip had so completely repudiated her.

But gradually another view of the matter suggested itself to her. She began to wonder about the exact nature of the attraction that had brought her here. Was it the force of the man, as much as the vision of the artist, that had drawn her to him? And she remembered the almost overpowering longing she had felt, that second day at the exhibition, to throw herself into his arms and burst into tears. Did he represent merely a refuge, she began to wonder, or was there also a strong sexual pull?

She tried to think of what her expectations had been during the journey, and had to admit that all the way along she had had a vision of herself falling into Miquel's arms and sobbing her heart out. Beyond that her imagination had not taken her. This was to be the end of her quest.

And it hadn't happened like that at all. Miquel had been kind, he had been caring, but he had lost no time in sending her off to bed where he had left her to do her crying on her own. Cry and sleep, those had been his orders – and she had been left alone to get on with both tasks. She had slept in his bed, she had been given a crumb of comfort in the warmth that his body had left in the sheets, but that was all. And his dictatorship had not ended there. When he discovered, two days after her arrival, that she had not told her husband where she was going, he had insisted that she should phone him. The thought of doing so had filled her with such dread that she had persuaded Miquel that it would do just as well if she were to phone her parents and tell them, on the understanding that they would contact Philip.

Altogether there was no doubt that Miquel was being slightly despotic.

Elise simply couldn't make up her mind as to what he felt for her. Sometimes she told herself that he was simply putting up with her incompetent and childish behaviour out of the kindness of his heart, and she didn't at all like this view of the matter. Then she reminded herself of the very personal interest he had shown on their second meeting, when he had been so aware of her sadness, and of the fact that he had been more or less expecting her to arrive here; and she comforted herself with the thought that she really must mean something to him.

But what the nature of that something was she would very much have liked to know. She was shocked to discover that there was a part of her that felt a certain disappointment. In spite of their living together in the same house, he had shown no indication of any sexual interest in her. Yes, she had to admit that she was disappointed, and surprised, and mortified. She had spent her adult life thinking of herself as a very attractive woman, and had been given every reason to think this. Why then did this man seem so impervious to her charms?

She decided to sound him out tactfully.

'How long do you think I should stay here?' she asked one day.

'I've told you before. Just as long as you wish. It's your life, it's your decision.'

'Decisions aren't always easy to make.'

'I suspect you are rather out of practice. When last did you make a decision, an important one, apart from deciding to come here?'

'I don't know. I really don't know. Perhaps I am out of practice. It didn't seem to be a problem before.' She thought of the certainty and confidence with which she had decided some years ago, before she had even met him, that Philip was the man she wanted to marry. She now thought of how she had approached him, how she had recovered from his initial rebuff and written to him, and it seemed almost impossible that she had ever had the confidence to behave like this.

But that had been the natural thing for her to do then, living as she had been in her intuitive world.

'I think I'm suffering from a loss of intuition,' she said. 'I used to know, yes, I really used to *know*, without any problem. And now everything seems so complicated.'

'You have spent too long trying to live by someone else's

standards. You must learn how to recognize and live up to your own.'

The conversation had not gone the way she intended. She had been hoping for some declaration from him that would show how much he cared, some indication that he actually wanted her to stay. But he had offered no such comfort. On the other hand, he had given her much to think of.

Later that day she came back to the same subject.

'You said I should make my own decisions. How does that fit in with the idea of flowing?'

'It's a case of making your own decisions in the light of what you actually feel, what you know intuitively, rather than trying to fit in with some preordained set of rules, your own or anybody else's. This is what you have been trying to do, and this is what has damaged you. And that is why you were so sad.'

After a pause he went on. 'And that is why I am not going to tell you what to do. Why I am not going to try to influence you – about going, or staying, or about the terms on which you stay.'

That night she went to bed feeling angry with him.

Why did he not give her some sign?

Did he really not care?

Why was he so determined that she was to make the first move?

For she now saw clearly that the decision in front of her was whether they were to become lovers or not, and she felt sure he must see this too. She had come round to accepting the view that from the start she had wanted him, even though she had no idea of this at the time. But realizing this and actually doing something about it were two very different things. How much simpler it would be, she thought, if he would just take her in his arms and carry her off to bed, freeing her from the difficulty of having to make a decision. Freeing her from the danger of having to accept a rebuff.

That was it, she now realized. The heart of the matter was simply this, that she was afraid to make the first move in case he rejected her. And once again she remembered her unthinking courage in advancing upon the unsuspecting Philip with her rose and her innocent confidence. This time her confidence had gone. And she didn't even have a rose to keep her company. She lay in bed that night, restless and dissatisfied with herself and with him. At last she sat up in bed and swung her feet down on to the floor. The cold of the tiles sent a little thrill through her, and she stood up proudly. Without a rose, she thought, without even a rose for company.

She walked along the corridor, opened his bedroom door and stood listening. Not a sound. Either he was asleep and hadn't heard, or else he was listening, waiting for her to speak, to move closer. It seemed that she was to be given no help, not till she was utterly committed. She wondered what would happen if she were to go back to her room now. It struck her that he might say nothing, and that she would never know whether he had been aware of her presence or not. And this unresolved question would lie between them from then on. No, she thought, she mustn't allow that to happen.

She advanced and sat down on the side of the bed. 'Miquel,' she whispered.

In silence he drew her into the bed beside him, holding her close. Then he gave a great sigh and said, 'I thought you would never come!'

Once again she lay in Miquel's bed, crying. But this time he was lying beside her, caressing her, and she realised that her recurrent longing to throw herself into his arms and burst into tears represented more than a need of comforting. It was also a symbol of a purely sexual desire to give herself to him in a total yielding.

The following morning Mme Marais shook her head once again over Elise's unmade bed. She made it up carefully as usual, reflecting on the fact that the week she had given them was nearly up. Perhaps I was wrong, she thought. But the next day, when she looked into the bedroom and found the bed untouched she nodded with satisfaction and muttered, '*Enfin!*' Then she advanced triumphantly and tore off the sheets.

There were no difficulties about the divorce. Each partner felt repudiated by the other, and the thing they both wanted more than anything else was to have the whole matter settled.

Some time after after the divorce Elise became pregnant, and they decided to marry. The marriage was not a thing that either of them had taken for granted. Elise was trying hard to follow Miquel's philosophy of flowing, and was aided in this by her natural tendency to act spontaneously. Gradually she was getting back to a more relaxed way of looking at life, trusting her intuition once again. And her intuition was telling her very clearly that she could best live her life beside Miquel, in spite of the insecurity of the situation. So she tried not to think about the future, and to accept each day as it came. But the prospect of having a child forced both of them to think along different lines.

Miquel had always been a free agent and had assumed that this was how he would remain for the rest of his life. But he felt that the claims of the unborn child must be taken into account. In a long discussion with Elise he explained that, for the child's sake he was willing to sacrifice his freedom – to a certain extent at least.

'That means you are prepared to give both me and the

child the security of marriage, but you don't intend to consider yourself as tied in any other way?'

'Yes, that's just about it.'

'But you wouldn't have considered giving me that security if it hadn't been for the child?'

'No. You don't need it. As far as our relationship is concerned, a legal obligation could add nothing. In fact, it might even spoil things completely. I think this is what marriage usually does. Compulsion spells the death of spontaneity. And that is why I said I was willing to sacrifice my freedom – which is our freedom – only to a certain extent. That will give us a chance to survive the marriage.'

Elise didn't ask what lines the freedom he intended to keep ran along. She assumed she could take it for granted that he was thinking of possible affairs with other women. She wondered whether he was prepared to grant her a similar amount of freedom, but decided against asking him. After all, she simply couldn't imagine herself ever again having the slightest interest in another man. What was the point of starting a possible argument over a situation that would never arise? She tried hard to convince herself that his view was right, that their hope for an untroubled relationship lay in this freedom clause; but the insecure, doubting part of her couldn't quite get rid of the notion that the proposed marriage was really her guarantee for the future.

And so they were married, very quietly, with only a few friends present, among whom was Mme Marais. It had taken Elise rather more than the prophesied week to warm to the woman, partly because of the language difficulty. Elise's school French seemed to be lacking in all the relevant vocabulary, and she had problems at first with the famous *accent du Midi*. But Elise learned quickly, and soon the two women were able to chat freely and laugh joyfully at the odd inevitable howler.

After some of their conversations Mme Marais would go off to continue with her work, shaking her head and murmuring in tones of approval, '*Elle apprend vite, celle-là*,' and Elise would be left wondering about the implied comparison. The Frenchwoman had accepted Elise's presence in such a matter-of-fact manner that it was difficult not to come to the conclusion that there had been other additions to the household of a similar nature. She was unwilling to broach the subject with Miquel, in case he felt she was jealous – well, was she? she wondered – and she certainly wasn't going to make any inquiries, either of Mme Marais or anyone else. But the implied suggestion that there had been others in the same position, along with Miquel's stipulation about his freedom in marriage, made her think often of how little she and this man she was sharing her life with knew about each other. What surprised her most was the fact that she was able to accept this uncertainty without letting it spoil the peace and happiness of her present life. Perhaps I'm learning to flow, she thought with a smile. Perhaps it's not only French that I'm making progress in.

Miquel devoted a great part of the day to working in his studio, and Elise liked to sit beside him, watching him paint. She was diffident about this at first, but soon realized that he really could get on with his work just as well when she was there. He spoke seldom, but would turn round often to exchange a smile with her or give her a fleeting kiss.

Shortly after they were married he started painting in a different way. He was still painting landscapes, but the figures seen against this background now held the centre of the stage. Instead of being sketched in lightly, as was the man in Elise's 'Homecoming' painting, each figure was drawn in great detail. The same effect of almost unearthly light was there, but now instead of being diffused throughout the landscape it was concentrated on the central figure. Sometimes it almost gave the effect of an aureole.

'Who's that?' asked Elise one day, looking at his latest picture. 'Is it one of the saints?'

'Almost. It's Blanquerna.'

'And who is Blanquerna?'

'It's the name of the central character in one of Ramon Llull's books – his most famous book, in fact. I don't suppose you've heard of Llull, have you?'

Elise shook her head.

'He was a mediaeval writer – Catalan, of course, you could guess by the name – who wrote books on philosophy, theology, mysticism, all sorts of subjects, always with the aim of spreading the Christian faith, especially among the infidels, which at that time in Spain meant the Moors with their Mohammedan faith. He travelled all over the place, including North Africa, preaching the gospel, writing all the time. And *Blanquerna* is the story of a particularly holy man.'

'Who really lived?'

'No. Llull invented him.'

'So the book is a novel?'

'Yes, more or less. One of the very first.'

'And why are you so interested in this character?'

'Because he was a wonderful man, and it's a splendid book, a luminous book. You should read it – in Catalan, of course.'

'Of course,' she replied, smiling. 'I only wish I could, if you think so much of it.'

That evening he came and sat down beside her, holding a book in his hand. 'I'm going to read it to you, in Catalan, and translate as we go along. How will you like that?'

'Lovely. I want to know what it is that you find so special about the book. Have you always liked it?'

'All my life. Since childhood, I think it's the book that has most influenced me. And I can hardly explain why. It's written from the orthodox Catholic point of view, which you know I don't share, and yet there's something about it, a sort of spiritual radiance, that enchants me.'

'A bit like your painting. There's a spiritual radiance there too.'

'And a simplicity, and clarity, and lack of clutter to which I cannot hope to aspire. It's like the paintings of Fra Angelico put into words. *Blanquerna* is a marvellous, resplendent antidote to our complicated and self-conscious modern world. There is this wonderful, liberating certainty that Llull feels and manages to communicate. And even though I can't believe in the dogmas that he preaches, the light shines through. And it's that, this radiance of his, that I should like to be able to communicate.'

So he read to her about Evast and Aloma and their son Blanquerna, and the dismay of the parents when he tells them he means to go off into the wilds to live as a hermit. And he read of how Aloma asks Natana, the beautiful and virtuous daughter of one of her friends, to try and persuade Blanquerna to marry her.

'What a lovely name, Natana!' exclaimed Elise.

'You like it?'

'Don't you?'

'Yes. But then, there's something very special, almost holy, about everything in this book, for me at least.'

'Miquel, I was just thinking, if it's a girl . . . '

'We could call her Natana?'

Elise smiled. 'What do you think?'

'I think it's a marvellous idea.'

'Let's go on. I want to know whether Natana succeeds.'

'Whether she gets her man, you mean?'

'Well, does she?'

'No. She has a greater success than that. Blanquerna inspires her to embrace the religious life.'

This answer left Elise feeling very thoughtful. After the reading was over for the evening she came back to this subject.

'Am I to take it that you think the religious life is better than marriage and family?'

'I think it's a higher calling.' Then, seeing a troubled look on her face he burst out laughing. 'Don't worry, I'm not good enough to go off into the wilderness. I like the good things of this world too much. Especially women.' He smiled as he saw her rueful expression on being given this ambiguous comfort. 'Especially you,' he added.

Elise smiled back. 'I'm trying to live in the present,' she said.

'How does it work? Are you happy?'

'Yes,' she answered, putting one hand on the bulge below her waist. 'I've never been so happy in my life.' And then she thought of the bliss of the first year of her marriage to Philip, and wondered whether she should qualify the statement. She said nothing, but kept on thinking about the question. In the end she decided that the extra quality there had been in her earlier happiness had lain in the fact that she was persuaded that it would last for ever. Now she suspected that all happiness is strictly provisional.

'You know,' she said to Miquel, 'I used to think that once you'd got what you wanted, that was it. You had it for good, and no further effort was needed. Happiness was assured.' She knew she wouldn't have to explain the train of thought that had brought her to this conclusion.

'And now you've learned that happiness is effort,' he replied.

'And that's why you keep on painting, isn't it?'

'One of the reasons. There's also the feeling that one has to contribute – whatever one has to contribute.'

'It makes me quite envious, sometimes. I have nothing to give.'

'You have a great deal to give to me. And to the world at large you have Natana to give – or Blanquerna, as the case may be.'

Natana grew up with virtually two mothers, for Mme Marais took as active a part in bringing up the child as did Elise. Miquel and Elise used to joke about it, saying that she had taken over the role of honorary grandmother.

She had been left a widow in her youth, with three young children to look after, and had managed to earn a living for them all by acting as housekeeper, cook, cleaner, or whatever else was required throughout the area. And then, when Miquel settled in the town, she had gradually withdrawn from her other commitments in order to give all her time to him. At first he thought it might have had something to do with the honour of working for the 'foreign painter'; but eventually he came to see that he had inspired in her a loyalty that verged on unquestioning adoration.

This sentiment she was prepared to transfer to whatever lover happened to be sharing Miquel's life at any given moment – and there had been many of them. Whether it was because Elise was also a foreigner, and therefore qualified for extra reverence, or because of her personal qualities, the fact was that Mme Marais took her to her heart almost as passionately as she had done with Miquel. And when the child arrived all this joint devotion was laid at the tiny feet of little Natana.

So Natana grew up fluent in French and English and, like most intelligent children in this situation, had no difficulty in distinguishing the forms of the one language from those of the other. In everything she was like her father, with the same dark, sturdy good looks, and the same confident, independent nature. From the start Natana knew what she wanted, just as she knew how to set about getting it with maximum co-operation from everyone else. She had her father's charisma and his energy.

From both parents she inherited a belief in the reality and importance of the unseen world. As a child she often told of encounters with strange beings which did not seem to fit into any of the accepted categories – not fairies nor elves, not satyrs nor naiads. Her parents accepted this without surprise – to Elise it seemed that these beings must be the near relations of the protagonists of the Celtic stories of her childhood, which you pretended to disbelieve but which you suspected everybody really did believe in. Miquel accepted these presences with an open mind, seeing them as possible forerunners of the world of myth and legend that was so important to him.

It was Mme Marais who was shocked and disturbed by the phenomenon. She could only imagine these strange beings as creations of the Devil, and would cross herself every time Natana said she had just seen the man with the flaming ears or the little green lady who sat under the tree at the far end of the garden.

Miquel was so captivated by the description of this little green lady that he painted a realistic picture of that part of the garden, with the little figure sitting under the tree. Natana looked at it critically.

'Well,' said her father, 'have I got it right?'

'*Pas mal, pas mal du tout. Mais la mienne est plus jolie.*' Natana usually spoke French when she had an opinion to offer or a decision to make. For her it seemed to be the language of evaluation.

Miquel looked at Elise with amusement. 'I seem to

have passed,' he said. 'But I obviously don't rate a distinction.'

He had intended the picture to be for family display only, but Elise persuaded him to include it in his next collection. The critics thought highly of it, spoke of the new direction of the artist's work, and had a field day interpreting the esoteric significance of the strange little figure. For some it represented the Unknown, for others it was the Spirit of the Earth, while one of the pundits insisted that it was the artist's subconscious.

'I'd like to think my subconscious was anything like as attractive as that,' was Miquel's comment.

Life was punctuated by Miquel's absences in different parts of Europe and America. The occasion was always the opening of one of his exhibitions. But there were times when the absence was longer than expected, and Elise knew, even before he told her, that there had been another woman involved. At first she was always terribly upset about this straying from the conjugal path. Mme Marais, without overtly referring to the situation, managed to administer her drop of comfort.

'Some people need change, in everything. He's always been like that. But when it's all over – the exhibition, I mean – he'll be so happy to come back, to you and to the child. And he will settle down again, and paint like a man possessed.'

'Till the next time.'

'Till the next time, *bien entendu.* He is like that. An artist.' That, in her opinion, summed up the whole matter.

And Elise learned to accept this view, and grew to feel less downcast every time he went away, knowing he would no doubt stray from her, but knowing just as certainly that he would come back. She sometimes wondered how long their relationship would have lasted had it not been for

Natana. Whatever happened, he would be sure to come back for her.

On one occasion, when Miquel had come home as soon as the exhibition was over, Elise and Mme Marais were commenting on this.

'It's Natana who draws him back,' said Elise.

'Natana and you,' corrected the older woman. Then she added, with a twinkle. 'And me too, perhaps – *un tout petit peu?*'

Elise laughed. 'More than just a little,' she said. 'You're really his first love.'

'*Que voulez-vous?* He likes my cooking. And I like to know I am playing my part. Not one of his paintings but would be the poorer without my cuisine. *C'est déjà quelque chose, n'est-ce pas?*'

8

So Philip was waiting for the second visit of the grown-up Natana. He was roused from his trance-like state by the doorbell, and jumped up and opened the door.

Natana stood there, holding a pink rose in her hand. With a slightly bashful smile she held the flower out to him. He took it from her, astonished and almost overcome by the memories it aroused.

'It's not coincidence,' she said, 'it's quotation.'

'So your mother told you about the rose?'

'Yes, she told me about the rose she tried to woo you with, and how you rejected it.'

'Well, I haven't rejected this one.' Philip had recovered his self-control. 'Let's go and get something to put it in.'

He led her into the kitchen.

'How tidy!' she remarked.

'It's a Mrs Wells day.'

'Ah, yes. The lady who took the book.'

'I'm afraid I haven't got started on preparing a meal. I've found it very difficult to concentrate on anything during the last twenty-four hours. But there's plenty of food in the freezer. I'm sure we can fix up something.'

'I'm sure I can, anyway, if there's any food at all in the house. I'm very resourceful, and totally unhampered by any formal training.'

'In the art of cooking?'

'In anything, I'm afraid. I do things spontaneously.'

'Your mother's daughter.'

'And my father's. Shall we get on with the meal and get that out of the way, and then I can answer all your questions, and you can answer mine?'

'Yours?'

'There's a lot I want to know about your life during the past twenty years or so. Your second marriage, for instance.'

'That wasn't exactly a success story either. But you're right, let's get on with the meal, and we can talk later.'

Natana was an inventive and uninhibited cook. She soon had the whole operation under control. Philip found himself obeying her orders and enjoying the experience, carried along by her enthusiasm.

At the end of the meal she asked, 'Is tomorrow a Mrs Wells day?'

'No, I'm afraid not.'

'Then we'd better get on with the clearing up. Where's your washing-up liquid?' Philip had intended to leave things till after she had gone, so that they could get on with their conversation, but decided that doing something with Natana, no matter what, probably involved less effort than leaving it undone against her will.

'You're not really very like your mother, are you?'

'Not in appearance, anyway.'

'No, nor in character.'

'Meaning?'

'She was less . . . '

'Less bossy, you mean?'

'I didn't quite mean to put it that way.'

'And so you were stuck for words. I know I'm bossy. My father always said so. And he knew what he was talking about.'

'You mean he was bossy too?'

'Yes. A sort of benevolent tyrant. An enlightened one, too. He almost forced you to do the right thing, when you couldn't or wouldn't see it. I'm probably trying to do the same thing – as in this washing-up business – but without his wisdom. So I just come over as bossy. But my motivation is the same as his.'

'Yes, I see that. I may not have wanted to do the washing-up just now, but I should have hated it even more after you'd gone. So I retract the word "bossy".'

'Which in fact you didn't use.'

'No, I allowed you to say it instead. That's the essence of diplomacy.'

'Now,' said Natana as soon as they were settled in the sitting room, 'tell me what you thought when the book arrived.'

'I simply didn't know what to think. And I was fairly reluctant to read it. But my friend Clive insisted that whoever had left it would no doubt come back to get my opinion. So I thought I'd better read it, in spite of serious misgivings. What would you have done if I hadn't read it?'

'I think I'd have cried at you.'

'Natana! You wouldn't do such a thing!'

'Not in cold blood. But I'd have been so disappointed that it would have been very difficult not to cry. And hardly worth the effort, all things considered.'

'Because you think your tears would have achieved something?'

'They might have. Or am I wrong?'

'Yes, I expect they might have. Which is a pretty sorry state of affairs, isn't it?'

'I don't know about that,' she said almost defensively. 'What's wrong with emotion?'

'Nothing, I suppose.' Philip spoke with little conviction. 'But it can be used as blackmail.'

'Perhaps, yes. But an innocent sort of blackmail in this case. You could almost call it whitemail. Anyway, you did read the book. That's the bit that matters.'

'I did, but only just. After I'd finished the first chapter I threw the thing into the wastepaper basket. It was fished out by Mrs Wells. Look!' He picked up the book and took the note out of it.

Natana laughed. 'That's lovely! Was this Meant, with a capital M. Out of the mouths of babes and sucklings! Mummy would have been convinced that it was Meant, with a capital M, that you should read the book, and that was why Mrs Wells was prompted to rescue it.'

'Mrs Wells would have rescued any book she had found in the wastepaper basket. I don't think she's a reader, but she has a great respect for things, perhaps even Things with a capital T.'

'Great! But Mrs Wells and her propensities were simply there, waiting in the wings, as it were, to rescue the book at the appropriate moment. You can't prove that wasn't part of the plan.'

'The Plan with a capital P?'

'Now you're laughing at me. And at my mother. And that's worse. *De mortuis*, etc.'

Philip's mood suddenly darkened. 'I just can't believe she's dead. And I don't know how you can speak so . . . so serenely, so almost lightheartedly, about it.'

'It's only temporary, after all.'

'Death, temporary? I thought that was the one thing we were all agreed about – the permanence of death.'

'If you've read my mother's book you must realize that she took a different view. She was sure that we'll all meet up again.'

'In the afterlife, I suppose.'

'In one of them, at any rate.'

'Natana, don't tell me you believe in reincarnation?'

'I don't see how one can afford not to believe in it.'

'Certainly I can quite see that it's a very comforting belief. But the fact that this would be a desirable state of affairs doesn't make it any the less false.'

'What's false about it?'

'The fact that it can't be proved.'

'I'm not at all sure that this follows.'

'You're not going to tell me you think it can be proved?'

'No, of course not. But, by the same token, it can't be *dis*proved. The mere fact that a thing can't be proved doesn't mean it's false. And anyway, it doesn't matter.'

'How can you of all people say it doesn't matter? I should have thought that it did matter terribly to anyone with your beliefs.'

'It's the proving and the disproving that don't matter, not the question of the afterlife. I don't need proofs, I just know it's there.'

'But how can you know, if you have no proofs?'

'Do you need a certificate before you can believe anything? Can't you take anything on trust?'

'Who on earth can one trust in such a matter, when nobody actually knows?'

'You can trust yourself, your intuition.'

Philip shook his head in perplexity. 'Look, Natana, we'll get nowhere along these lines. All I can say is that you're terribly, terribly like your mother.'

'I'm sure that, in this context, that's not meant as a compliment. But I'm glad I'm like her, anyway.'

'You've got the same beliefs, and the same infuriating way of mixing logical argument with unacceptable premises. But she was gentler when she argued. You do it with more verve and passion.'

'Which makes it easier for you.'

'Does it?'

'Yes. You don't need to feel such a heel when you disagree.'

There was a silence, which Philip broke with the sudden question, 'Tell me, why did your mother walk out on me?'

'Because you had rejected her.'

'What do you mean, rejected her? I did nothing of the sort.'

'Don't tell me you didn't go and sleep in another room, without even telling her you were going to?'

'Do you call that rejecting her?'

'What would you call it? To shut yourself away from her, in another room, without a word of explanation? I can't think of a more explicit symbol of rejection than that.'

'It wasn't meant as that. It was merely a way of showing how much she had hurt me by the way she had behaved. It was she who rejected me, going off after that, without telling me.'

'She left a note.'

'Yes, a stupid, ambiguous little note. "I'm going home," it said. Naturally I took it that she had gone to her mother's. And I did nothing about it for two days. And then I rang her parents and discovered she wasn't there. You can imagine what we all thought the going-home bit meant, after that. And I had phoned the police and they had started a search, when she phoned from Perpignan. Going home, my God! When she had gone off to a country she had never even been in before! What did she mean by it?'

'She meant that she had recognized in my father's painting something of her spiritual home. The fact that you'd lived beside her for four years and hadn't understood this simple fact, that she just didn't live in your materialistic, verifiable world, shows how right she was to go.'

'We were ill matched,' he admitted sadly. 'And yet at

first . . . I don't know what went wrong. We were very happy for a year or two.'

'Yes, I know. And that was why she felt bad about having left you, and wanted to make it up to you the only way she could, with her book. And my father agreed, and helped her and encouraged her. He was a generous man.'

Philip was nodding his head thoughtfully. 'Tell me more about him. Were they happy together?'

'Yes, very happy. Most of the time. He wasn't altogether faithful to her. He would go off, always when he had an exhibition somewhere abroad, and he would stay away much longer than he need have. And Mummy knew, and I learned later, that there was usually another woman involved. It made her very unhappy, especially at first. But, apart from that, they were very happy together. I think they were ideally suited to each other. She gave him stability, and the joy of family life, which he hadn't known before. And he taught her that you can be happy with someone without owning them.'

Philip took in this last statement with a slight sense of shock. Was the girl preaching at him? Or was she just referring to Elise's attitude during her first marriage? He had to admit that both he and Elise had taken it for granted that marriage meant possession. He made a mental note that this was something he would do well to think about later on.

'And you? Did you have a happy childhood?' he asked.

'Very. All my life has been happy. The only sorrows I've had have been the death of my parents. And even in that I've been luckier than some, because I've not been left alone. I've still got Mme Marais.'

'And who is this lady?'

'She had been my father's housekeeper for years, and she stayed on after Mummy arrived on the scene. I look on her as my second mother, and she's still with me. I inherited the house and enough money to live on, so we just mean to stay on there.'

'So you're going back to Perpignan?'

'Yes – are you sorry?' she asked disconcertingly.

'Well, yes, I am. It's nice having you here. When are you going back?'

'I've no idea. When I've finished my business here.'

'And what does your business here consist of?'

'It consists of teaching you to love my mother again.'

'Natana, you don't know what you're saying!'

'I do. That is what I'm here for.'

'Look, I can understand that you feel you must carry out your mother's intentions in seeing to it that I read the book. And I can see that you'll feel you have carried out your commission better if you can make me accept what is in the book. But I can't see what possible gain is to be had from trying to teach me to love your mother again. She's dead, Natana. My love can't reach her.'

'I'm not so sure about that. But the important thing about your loving her again is what this can do for you.'

Philip had an uncomfortable suspicion that the girl might be right, but he fought against it. 'For over twenty years I've been trying to forget your mother. And I had succeeded pretty well, till you came along. I had to forget her, that was the only way to make the whole thing bearable.'

'Yes, I can see that. But all this happened twenty years ago. It looks as if you're still stuck in the same place. Mummy went through a stage like that as well, she told me. And I suppose it was easier for her to grow out of it, because she had my father's help. That was the good thing about his marital infidelities. He didn't expect any jealousy on my mother's part and he didn't feel any either.'

'You mean, your mother . . . ?'

'No. Nothing like that. It was retrospective jealousy, I

meant. And that was why he was able to help Mummy so much, when she wanted to do something for you. He helped her with the book, and, above all, he encouraged her in her idea. He knew it would be a form of healing for both of you.'

'Healing? After all these years?'

'Are you suggesting it isn't necessary?'

Philip said nothing. He was becoming aware of the armour of insensitivity that he had built round himself. The contrast between this rigidity and Natana's free, flowing way of looking at life had become quite painful. After a moment of silence he remembered something that suddenly seemed appropriate.

'I've just remembered. The night before last, when I was still waiting for your first visit, I had a dream. I dreamt your mother was standing in front of me. I can remember nothing else, simply that she was there. And I hadn't dreamt of her in years. Make what you can of that.'

'You can imagine what I'll make of it. And what do you make of it? Sheer coincidence?'

'Of course.'

'Predictable. But thank you for telling me, anyway. That was generous of you.'

It was a great relief to Philip to get this little bit of praise from Natana. He felt that so far he had not come well out of the conversation.

The bell rang and Philip went to open the door. Clive was standing there.

'I knew there was no point in expecting you to come and see me this week, in case you missed the visitation. So I thought I'd just drop in. Any signs of the mysterious young lady?'

'Yes, she's here. Come through and meet her.'

As they walked along the passage to the sitting room

Philip felt a slight sense of unease which he couldn't quite explain to himself. It wasn't that he intended to keep anything from Clive, after all. Perhaps it was just that he wanted Natana to himself – for the time being, at least, till they had cleared up the backlog of things to be discussed between them.

'Natana, this is Clive.'

'Oh, how nice! I've heard a lot about you.' Natana spoke with evident pleasure, and this added to Philip's vague sense of unease and annoyance.

'Really? I wonder what this man's been saying about me?'

'Actually, I knew all about you long before I met Philip.'

'From whom?'

'My mother.'

Seeing the surprise on Clive's face, Philip intervened.

'Natana is Elise's daughter,' he said curtly, and was almost pleased to see his friend disconcerted by the information.

'Indeed?' Clive seemed rather at a loss. 'And how is your mother?'

'Dead. Dead but well, or so I understand.'

She's outrageous, thought Philip. She wants to startle and shock these two old fogeys, I can see that. But why? Is it just a power game? He was reluctant to believe this. He found the girl so attractive, both in her personality and in her person, that he wanted to find some more acceptable reason than mere mischief-making in some of her more uncomfortable sallies.

After a pause Clive recovered. 'Well, that was quite a conversation-stopper,' he admitted. 'But, on consideration, it seems to fit in with your plugging a book on the occult. If, as it appears, you are in contact with your mother, do give her my kindest regards, or best wishes, or whatever is appropriate for the sphere of life, or should I say death, to which she has been called.'

Philip was a little annoyed by Clive's aggressive tone. He wouldn't have dared to speak to Natana like this, in spite of the fact that he so completely shared Clive's point of view. There seemed to be something almost improper in Natana's determination to include the afterlife in their conversation; but he certainly wouldn't wish to speak to her in the overtly mocking voice that Clive had adopted.

But Natana took it in good part. 'I'll do my best. She often spoke of you, and of your wife, as good friends. And she was sorry to hear of her death.'

'Yes, that happened just after your mother – left, shall we say? It was precisely the day she left that we learned that what we had taken to be a mild indisposition was in fact leukaemia.'

'And she died quite soon, didn't she?' Natana had evidently overlooked the hostile intent on Clive's part, and was regarding him with sympathy.

'Yes. A matter of weeks. And, unfortunately, unlike you and your mother, we don't seem to have managed to establish any form of two-way communication. Perhaps you could give me the recipe.' It would have been hard to assess the degree of bitterness in Clive's voice. Clearly this was more than lighthearted banter.

For answer Natana picked up the book that was lying on the coffee table beside her.

'My mother's book,' she said. 'It might help you to get started.'

Clive was so startled at hearing that Elise was the author that he forgot all about his hostile intentions. 'You mean, Elise wrote that?' He turned to Philip. 'Can you believe this? I mean, I'm not doubting your word, Natana, but I must admit it's the last thing I would have predicted.'

'It's the last thing I would have predicted too,' Philip admitted. 'And yet, it does lie so completely within the sphere of her interests. Perhaps one of us, I at least, should have thought of it.'

Natana turned a pensive look on Philip, and gave him a little smile. He's coming on, she decided.

Meanwhile Clive had picked up the book and was turning over the pages. 'I say!' he exclaimed. 'This is really a bit much. I look up the bit on herbalism, thinking that sounds a reasonable sort of subject, with which a rational creature might not be too out of sympathy, and I find *The Doctrine of Signatures*. Philip, do you know what this means?'

'I do now. It's the belief that the appearance of a plant will tell you what it's supposed to be good for.'

'Precisely. With a quotation from Culpeper to give it respectability. "And by the icon or image of every herb, man first found out their virtues." Never heard such arrant nonsense.'

Philip felt much the same, but was reluctant to put his objections quite so baldly.

'You must admit,' he said to Natana, 'That it's a bit difficult for a reasonable, twentieth-century man to take that sort of thing seriously.'

'Yes, it must be difficult, if he's suffering from intuitive ineptitude. If you accept that the universe has a thinking mind behind it, then there's no problem. But I shouldn't for a moment suppose that either of you is prepared to concede the intentionality of the creation.'

Clive exploded. 'Natana, for God's sake, stop speaking like a stuffy old theologian. Where on earth did you get all these ideas? And, above all, why on earth is an attractive young woman like you bothering her head about them?' Clive sounded really exasperated.

Natana laughed. 'I think it's your head I'm bothering, not

mine. And I got the ideas from my parents. This was the sort of thing they often talked about. Would you rather we discussed the latest pop idols, or the political situation in the Middle East?'

By the time he left, half an hour later, Clive had come round to thinking that Natana was a very attractive and likeable young woman, even if a bit disconcerting. She had obviously been brought up with some very peculiar ideas. He couldn't help feeling that Philip was a lucky man, with a girl like that taking an interest in him.

'Tomorrow's Wednesday,' he reminded Philip just before leaving. 'See you for lunch at the staff club.'

'So it is! Time for my weekly dose of Academe. See you there.'

'Meanwhile, have fun.'

Once again Philip felt a faint current of disapproval run through him. Somehow, he and Clive just weren't on the same wavelength at all tonight. He dismissed the thought and went back to Natana.

'He doesn't seem to think much of my ideas, does he?' she asked.

'It's all you can expect from someone suffering, like me, from intuitive ineptitude. You must admit you do hit pretty hard at times.'

'So does he.'

'And I?'

She considered her reply for a moment. 'I think you're hitting less hard than you were.'

'Do you think you're taming me?'

'I wish I could think that.'

Suddenly Philip felt he was treading on dangerous ground. Either the girl was altogether too spontaneous and innocent for her own good, or else she was less naive than she seemed, in which case it might possibly be he who was in danger. He thought of how much she had filled his thoughts since their first meeting little more than twenty-four hours ago, and felt distinctly uncomfortable.

'Tell me more about your namesake in the mediaeval Catalan book.' He felt this should be a safe-enough subject, equally distant from philosophical speculation and from the question of their relationship.

'She was good and beautiful, and dutiful and intelligent. And she was supposed to marry the hero, to keep him from going off into the wilderness to be a hermit. But instead he talks her into becoming a nun, and she ends up as a particularly holy abbess.'

'You don't see yourself following her example?'

'Never. Nobody would be mad enough to make me an abbess. And I don't think I'd ever be mad enough to become a nun. I like men too much.'

Once again Philip was disconcerted. Was this an overture? What sort of a girl was this, anyway? An extremely liberated young woman of great sophistication, or a simple girl who had led such a protected life that she didn't know what dangers she was courting with her frank admissions? And then it struck him that neither of these pictures might be the right one. It could be that she thought of him as so old that there was no question of sexual provocation in her behaviour.

Natana spoke again, introducing a completely different subject.

'You haven't told me about your second marriage yet. Your wife is still alive, I take it?'

'So I believe.'

'You have no contact with each other, then?'

He shook his head.

'You know,' she said, 'I have a mental image of you carrying a ruler in your hand, ready to draw a straight, hard, very black line at the end of every relationship. I wish you'd throw that ruler away.'

'Why?'

'Because I think you'd be much happier without it. And also because I don't want to see the black line drawn under my name.'

'Oh, Natana, how could you think I'd do that?'

'You've done it twice before.'

'Only with my wives,' he said, half jokingly.

'I'll be all right so long as I don't marry you, you mean? But tell me about this other marriage. What was she called?'

'Davina.'

'That's a nice name.'

'Yes, there's nothing wrong with the name.'

Natana heaved a sigh.

'Right, then,' she said, 'go ahead and tell me what was wrong with the woman.'

'I suppose I now ought to say there was nothing wrong with her, really. That it was just a case of incompatibility. That would be the mature, understanding way of looking at it, wouldn't it?'

Natana was gazing at him with an ironic little smile.

'But that's not what you're going to say?'

'No. I'm going to tell you the truth instead. And the truth is that she's the hardest, coldest, greediest, most cynical bitch I've ever come across.'

'You don't beat about the bush, do you?'

'I'm learning from you.'

'Well, I'm listening. You can now start demolishing Davina.'

9

At the age of fourteen Davina had a vision. It was the first time she had experienced anything of the sort and it shaped the course of her whole life.

She was lying in bed one morning, managing to ignore her mother's repeated warnings about being late for school, when the thing happened. Later on, trying to describe the occurrence to herself, she could find no words for the experience beyond stating what she saw. And she saw it, she lay there watching it, as one watches a scene on the television screen. Only, the screen on this occasion was her bedroom ceiling.

What she saw took place in a sun-drenched street. She could see a bit of a white building that looked like part of an elegant American apartment block. In the foreground, next to the building, was a garage, with the door open. A smart sports car had just been driven out of the garage and was standing by the pavement with its engine purring expensively. Walking from the car to the garage was the figure of a young woman, tall, slim, casually elegant, almost arrogantly self-assured. The girl pressed a button at the side of the garage, and the door swung shut automatically. Then the girl turned and walked back to the car.

Her hair was long and straight, and of dark reddish brown, and she wore sunglasses of exactly the same shade. She carried a lighted cigarette in her hand, and had a large, bright green leather bag slung over her shoulder. She was wearing dark brown trousers with a waistcoat to match, and a cream blouse. The colour of her skin was a dark golden tan, her lips glaringly scarlet. The sunglasses hid the eyes, but Davina was certain that they too must be heavily made up.

And the face was the face of Davina.

Not as she was at present, of course. It was the face of Davina *in posse*.

She lay watching the vision, holding her breath with excitement, till the picture faded. Then she got out of bed and stood in front of the mirror, taking stock of the changes that would have to be made. The material was not promising. An immeasurable amount of effort would have to go into the venture. But the result would be absolutely mindblowing.

'Davina, if you don't get up now you'll miss the school bus. I'm not calling you again.'

'Okay, Mum, I am getting up.' To herself Davina announced solemnly that she was never again going to have to be called more than once. There was going to be no time to waste. She closed her eyes for a moment, trying to recapture the details of the girl's appearance. Looks about twenty-four, she decided. That gives me ten years. I think I can just make it.

And the first week of those ten years she dedicated to working out her plan. She decided on a two-pronged approach – her person and her mind were to be taken rigorously in hand. For a kick-off, no more Mars bars; no more soft drinks. As for the rest of the changes necessary to produce the long, elegant limbs and the slender, supple body, she would have to go to the library and consult the appropriate books. She had a suspicion that her mother's unenlightened views on nutrition might be in for a bit of a shock.

The cultivation of the mind was a matter she felt she could safely leave to her teachers for the time being. If she just got down to it, and did the work she was supposed to do, that would give her a basis on which she could build later on. Once she had caught up with the rest of the class she could then map out the lines along which her future studies should go. But she would need help. The best thing would be to consult Miss Shackles, the Deputy Head.

She was astonished by the fact that the prospect of all the work that lay before her didn't fill her with dread and discouragement. No task seemed too great, no timetable too crowded. She had had her vision. She knew where she was going.

'Yes, Davina? What is it?' Miss Shackles managed not to add the word 'now' to her question.

Davina stood in front of her and shifted uneasily from one foot to the other. No words came. Miss Shackles sighed. She knew the symptoms only too well.

'Who's sent you this time?' she asked, without looking up.

'Nobody, miss.'

Miss Shackles looked up.

'Then what are you doing here?'

'I just wanted to consult you, miss.'

'Consult?' The teacher looked up in surprise and really saw the girl for the first time. It was such an unexpected word for Davina to use that the woman stared at her intently.

'Is something the matter?'

'No, miss.'

'Then what d'you want to consult me about?'

'About my future.'

'Ah!' Miss Shackles showed her astonishment. If asked,

she would probably have opined that Davina didn't have a future.

'Well, if you want to have any sort of a future you'll have to start working, that's all I can say.'

'I am working, miss. You can ask Mrs Potter, my form-mistress. I've been working for a whole week.'

Miss Shackles looked up with a seldom-seen twinkle in her eye.

'That's quite a feat, is it?'

'Yes, miss. For me it is.'

'I should think that's quite a realistic assessment. I'll tell you what, Davina. If you keep on working hard for another month, you can come back and see me again, and we'll have a talk about your future. How will that do?'

'Yes, miss,' replied Davina with impenetrable stolidity.

Miss Shackles watched the lumpy figure leave the room and wondered what she would ever be able to say to the girl about her future that would be neither depressing nor untrue. Job in a factory, she thought; supermarket checkout; at best working in a hairdresser's, if she does something about her appearance. Poor lamb, she doesn't stand much of a chance. One of the world's losers, if ever I saw one. Nothing going for her. Not even a pleasant manner.

Davina was not ill pleased with the outcome of the interview. Another month of hard work would have consolidated her position in her various classes, so there would be good reports coming in. And after that, she thought, I'm off. There'll be no stopping me.

A month later Davina stood in front of Miss Shackles once again, armed with a number of notes from her surprised teachers, all of them stating that she had been working very well lately.

'Well, Davina, you do seem to have made a dramatic

improvement. Can you tell me what has turned you into such a reformed character?'

'I suppose it's just part of the process of growing up, miss,' was the demure reply.

'I see.' Miss Shackles didn't see at all. A month ago she would have guessed that the only thing that a girl like Davina would be able to see in the process of growing up was sex. 'Now, then, what sort of a job were you thinking of aiming at?'

'I don't really know, miss. But I know what I want. I want a job with responsibility, and proper training, and travel, and lots and lots of money. I want to be someone, for a change. I want to be able to wear nice clothes and drive a fast car and have clever friends and . . . and be respected, that's what I want.' She could have added that she also wanted to be slim and beautiful and infinitely desirable, but she kept that part of the dream to herself.

'I see.' This time the teacher did see, and was amazed at the girl's frankness. She felt sure this was the dream of most of the school's pupils; but not one, in all her years of teaching, had ever stated her ambition so clearly and frankly. She realized there must be a very strong motivation here, to have helped the girl to break the barrier of silence.

'Now, let's see. We ought to build on your abilities. Which subjects are you good at?'

'None of them, miss.'

'Don't you think, then . . . ?'

'No, miss, I don't think it's a waste of time, if that's what you were going to say. I can work. I can work harder than the lot of them put together, even the clever ones. I'm even getting my spelling right. I'm not clever enough to be dyslexic, so that's no problem.'

Miss Shackles sent a probing look across the table. Was the girl taking the mickey? Davina looked at her with an expression of impenetrable seriousness. The teacher meditated for a moment.

'Computers, that's what it's got to be,' she announced at length.

'Yes, miss.'

'My brother's in computers, and he says that's where the future lies. Have you heard of micro-electronics?'

Davina shook her head.

'Well, it's going to transform our lives. By the time you've finished school there will be a huge demand for highly trained computer specialists. You could go to LSE.'

'What's that?' Davina thought it sounded like a drug.

'London School of Economics.'

'I'd rather go to university than another school.'

'It is a university.'

'Oh!'

That, as far as Davina was concerned, was that. The big decision had been made. All that was required now was to do well enough at school to be accepted by LSE, and in the course of time she would be turned loose on the market as a fully trained computer expert, with a variety of highly paid jobs to choose from.

But if life at school had become pleasanter and more stimulating, life at home was posing a bit of a problem. Her mother had not taken kindly to being informed that her menus were dietetically disastrous.

'You'll just eat what I give you, young lady. You needn't think I'm going to be wasting my time messing about with salads and all that nonsense. You can buy your own when you start work in a couple of years' time. Meanwhile you'll eat what I give you, and no nonsense.'

'I'm not going to start work in a couple of years' time. I'm going to get my A levels and then go to LSE.'

'To what?'

'LSE. London School of Economics.' She put all the scorn into her voice that her mother's ignorance merited.

'Oh, you are, are you? Who do you think you are, anyway, with your salads and brown bread and A levels? Lady Muck?'

Davina decided against arguing with her mother about the food. Instead of spending her pocket money on sweets she bought salads and yogurts and wholewheat bread, and ate as little as possible of the family fare.

The argument about staying on at school she put off till the time for a decision came. She won, thanks to her natural ruthlessness and a collection of surprisingly good school reports. Her parents were both annoyed and gratified, and decided they should perhaps start boasting about their clever daughter. Davina didn't care whether they boasted or not. She had already cut herself off from them in everything but physical presence.

When the time came for her to go to university in London she left her home with only one regret – the fact that, as long as she was a student, she would have to come back here for the vacations. After that she would really make an end.

And after her graduation, she determined, all ties must be broken.

At twenty-one she set off for her first job. Not quite California yet, but on the way, she told herself. It was with a big exporting firm in Liverpool. As she moved into her little flat she felt a surge of pride and triumph. She hadn't quite made it yet, but she still had three years in hand. And a small flat in the centre of Liverpool was already a far cry from a council estate on the outskirts of Sheffield.

As for her appearance, things were going well. She had got rid of the spots and puppy fat, she was tall and slim and supple. And now she would have more time to attend to the business of dress and make-up. She decided that it would be a good idea to follow a part-time course in modelling. Not that she thought of this as a career. If you were successful the money was good, and it must be nice to be paid to be beautiful and get all that admiration. But she wanted the admiration as a sort of non-professional perk. She felt she could make her mark better in the business world. She wanted admiration, but she wanted power too. And she wanted her success to last longer than the few seasons of tirumph that even a top model can hope for.

After two years of frequent promotion she was transferred to Los Angeles. I've made it, she thought. I've made it, with a year in hand.

Her triumphant arrival in LA was followed by a period of reaction.

In the first place, she spent a long time looking for an apartment that matched the one she had glimpsed on her bedroom ceiling, and in the end had to make do with a slightly different, though equally luxurious, version. This was the moment, she felt, to get herself the outfit she had been wearing in the vision. She couldn't find what she wanted in the shops, so she had it made, at enormous expense. That, of course, didn't matter. She could well afford it. She knew exactly what she wanted, and from now on she was going to see to it that she got it.

But she next discovered that getting exactly what she wanted never seemed to produce the satisfaction she had expected. Eventually she came to realize that, for the first time for many years, she had nothing to aim at. She had lost her motive power. Her years of hard slog had built up a habit that she now had difficulty in shaking off. She found herself spending much of her free time lying around, doing nothing, aimless and discontented. She hadn't been in LA long enough to have many friends; she could cope with her work easily – what more was there to do? One evening as she lay on her bed looking at the ceiling, wondering what to do next, she remembered how much of her time she had spent doing just that – before the revolution occurred in her life. She sat up suddenly, saying, 'No, not that. Never again.' And she set about finding ways to fill her life with some sort of challenge.

Once again she decided on a two-pronged attack. She was going to specialise further in her own branch of computer science, make herself an authority on the subject, and see how far she could climb in the administration of the firm she was in. The aim was to become general director. Not very realistic perhaps, especially for a woman, but still . . . She thought of how far she had come, and decided that this was just the sort of challenge she needed.

After two years she was sent back to England – to London this time. This fitted in very well with her plans. To be working in Head Office gave her the best possible opportunity to realize her ambitions, and it was a good place to continue her research.

And it was precisely at this point that she came across her first hitch. Just as both of her ambitious projects were getting on very nicely, a completely unforeseen disaster occurred. Davina fell in love, or something like it, and not only with one man, but with two; if not concurrently, at least in very quick succession.

Philip and Clive had decided just about this time that they really ought to do something to get out of the rut into which they felt they had slipped. It was five years since Elise had left and Myra had died, and both men had got used to their renewed bachelor-type existence. Neither found work particularly demanding, and both were becoming aware of the fact that all aspects of life, including scientific research, were becoming increasingly computerised. So they decided to go on an intensive course held by one of the university colleges for graduates in mathematics and the sciences. And on their very first day there they found themselves in a tutorial run by an extremely good-looking, intelligent and capable young woman.

Davina, as one of the more advanced PhD students of the college, had been asked to take on some of the tutorial work in this course. Teaching was something she had never done before, or thought of doing; but she set about it with her usual thoroughness and determination, and found she enjoyed the experience. It pandered to her sense of power. Here she was, explaining, assessing; judging. And her pupils were all graduates, some of them academics, all highly intelligent, all totally ignorant of the very subject she had at her finger tips. She found teaching absolutely intoxicating.

And among her students were these two interesting males in their early thirties, both good-looking, both highly presentable, and both evidently struck by her attractions.

So far Davina simply hadn't had time to notice that sort of thing. She had taken a number of lovers after she went to California, as the pressure was off – she had achieved her ambition. But she was only interested in them as sexual partners, and she had formed none but the most casual of relationships with any of the men involved. It could have been argued, and Davina did carry on the argument with herself for some days, that, with her renewed commitment to an unrealistically high ambition, she was once again in the position of having no time for that sort of thing. But for once common sense was unable to prevail.

For the first few days she was convinced she was in love with Clive. Then she began to waver. Perhaps it was really Philip she preferred. By the time the course was finished she had decided she was going to marry one of them, but wasn't quite sure which. She had so much enjoyed being the visible object of their homage – the rush to open doors, to bring her drinks, the envious looks of the other women, who obviously felt it was most unfair that Davina should have a monopoly on the two most presentable men on the course – that she thought it would be a good idea to assure herself this sort of attention for the rest of her life. Hence her decision to marry. Merely having an affair with the one or the other, or both, for that matter, would do nothing to guarantee the long-term position of superiority that marriage seemed to offer.

At the end of the course, faced with the decision of which suitor to choose, she decided on a sort of Trial by Ordeal. Since they seemed so well matched in all other respects, she would make her choice on the merits of the sexual prowess of each of the two candidates. And for this, of course, she would have to go to bed with both of them. Not at the same time, of course. For a moment she let her thoughts wander freely, then decided they were both far too conventional even to consider such a suggestion. No, it would have to be done separately. Whether the men would confide in each other she didn't know, and she didn't much care. She found it hard to imagine that either would have any scruples about going to bed with her merely because she had already done so with his friend. What, after all, are friends for, she asked herself with a cynical smile, if not to share in each other's joys and sorrows? No, they could tell each other or not, as they pleased. It would make no difference to her. And she felt under no obligation to reveal anything to either man. They were free agents, all three, and could do as they pleased.

After the double trial, she decided on Clive. She felt he just had the edge on Philip in bed, and besides, it would be rather nice to be a professor's wife. And it was widely rumoured that Clive would fall heir to the recently vacated chair in his own department. Yes, Clive was to be the happy man, and she would be Mrs Professor Bowen, as it were. For someone with her totally non-academic background, this would be glory indeed. It would be the third jewel in her crown, to add to those of her own academic achievements and her meteoric rise in the business world.

Having made her decision she wondered whether to wait for Clive to propose, manoeuvre him into proposing, or just settle the matter herself. She decided on the third option, as probably the simplest, and certainly the quickest. She was aware of the fact that she was spending a lot of time on this business, to the detriment of her other commitments, and wanted to get back to her normal life as soon as possible – everything as before, but with a husband in the background.

It was during their second night together that she decided to raise the subject. They were lying in bed, quiet with approaching sleep, when Davina said, 'Do you like being with me?'

'Mmmm!' he replied sleepily, and gave her ear a gentle bite.

'Then don't you think we should make it a permanent arrangement?'

'Move in with me? Or me with you? Why not? Your place or mine, eh?'

Davina began to suspect that the conversation had gone slightly off the rails. She abandoned her lateral approach and came out into the open, a position in which she felt far more at home.

'I was thinking we could get married.'

Suddenly Clive was wide awake. 'Oh! No, no. I'm sorry, I can't.'

'Why not? You told me your wife had died. Don't say you got married again?'

'Quite the opposite.'

Davina was rather literal-minded. 'I don't see what you mean. What's the opposite of getting married again?'

'Never getting married again.'

'But why not? Was your marriage so unhappy that it's put you off for life?'

'No. Again, quite the opposite. We were so happy, and we had so little time together, that we felt we'd both been cheated. And I swore I would never marry again. Because it would be unfair if I had more of the same type of happiness, when she had been denied it.'

'And you made her a promise not to marry again?'

'No. I made the promise to myself, for her sake.'

'But she's dead. You can do what you like now. After all, you've just been making love to me. What would she think of that?'

'I don't think she'd mind – not much, at any rate. She was a very sensible, realistic sort of a woman. She would realize I can't live like a monk.'

'So?'

'I promised myself, and I couldn't live at peace if I broke that promise. It's the least I can do in her memory.'

'Very well. There's nothing more to be said about it.'

Davina turned over on to her side and fell asleep.

The following morning she decided she would have to make do with second-best. It was the first time in many years that she had been forced into this position, but there was nothing she could do about it. She recognized that she was powerless to argue against the irrational, as she classified Clive's determination not to remarry.

She could, of course, give up the whole idea of marriage. But that would be tantamount to an even greater confession of failure. Besides, she felt that by marrying Philip she would have done something to show Clive that the loss was his, not hers.

The next night she embarked on a similar manoeuvre with Philip. Here the facts of the case worked in her favour instead of against her, for Philip was still smarting from the humiliation of having been abandoned by his wife. He was flattered by the thought that a woman as attractive and successful as Davina should wish to marry him, and had no difficulty in persuading himself that it would be an excellent arrangement.

Davina had been right in assuming that both men had a rather conventional outlook as far as sexual relations were concerned. Neither had mentioned to the other that he was the happy possessor of Davina's favours. The day after her unsuccessful proposal Clive would have liked to discuss the matter with Philip, but thought it would be disloyal to Davina. He felt bad enough about having refused her, and this would be adding insult to injury. But by the second day his desire to unburden himself had overcome his scruples, and he decided that he must tell Philip when they met at lunch. It's not often that a man gets the chance to turn down a woman like Davina, and he felt he had to tell someone. And that someone, of course, had to be Philip, his best friend.

They chatted about this and that, each looking for an opening to blurt out his piece of news. At last, after a pause, both started together, with a somewhat forced:

'By the way—'

Both paused.

'Go on.'

'No, you go on.'

'I just wanted to tell you that I'm going to marry Davina.'

Philip was expecting some surprise at the news, but he

certainly wasn't prepared for the sheer astonishment that his announcement produced. Feeling slightly uncomfortable at Clive's reaction, he then said, 'Well, what were you going to say?'

'Oh, nothing. Nothing. I can't really remember. But, I mean . . . congratulations, anyway.' He simply didn't know whether he ought to tell Philip the rest of the story or whether a discreet silence was called for. He knew he would have to think about it. Meanwhile, perhaps he could sound a word of caution, on general principles.

'I must say, I'm a bit surprised at your thinking of remarrying, after your first unhappy experience.'

'Ah, but this is so different. You know yourself what was the matter with my first marriage. We just lived in different worlds. And Elise's was a rarefied, unreal, indefinable and unpredictable world. We had nothing in common. It's different with Davina. You may not know her as well as I do, but you know her well enough to realize that her approach to life is very like ours – rational, realistic, cerebral.' He brought this last word out as a player throws down his ace of trumps. To be cerebral, it appeared, amounted to a total guarantee of happiness in marriage.

'And think of your marriage with Myra. Again those qualities. And I don't have to remind you of how well that marriage worked.' So, having produced two examples to illustrate his contention, Philip sat back, satisfied that he had examined the subject in all its ramifications.

Clive managed to hold back a sigh. Poor chap, he thought, he really must be in love. He felt somewhat sobered as he reflected that he himself had very nearly been in the same boat. Had it not been for his devotion to Myra's memory, he might by now be head over heels in love and mental confusion. There but for the grace of God, he thought, then reflected that this was an unsuitable phrase for a confirmed agnostic to have in his mind. He reworded the sentiment, telling himself he'd had a lucky escape.

Three days later he was still puzzling over whether to reveal his secret to Philip, when he had a phone call to say that they had just got married, and would he like to come round for a celebratory drink? Clive agreed, and set off in some despondency, blaming himself for his indecision. Now there was nothing for it but to let events take their course.

Clive thought there might be quite a jolly crowd there, but found he was the only guest. After a while Davina sent Philip to the kitchen to get some more ice. She turned to Clive with a slightly mocking smile.

'You're so alike,' she said.

'Really?'

'In everything,' she added.

10

Natana was looking at Philip with a mixture of amusement and sympathy.

'Poor Philip! It doesn't sound like a recipe for a happy marriage. When did you learn that she'd made the same offer to Clive?'

'Quite early on. It didn't take long for things to get really bad. It was Davina herself who told me, in a fit of pique. It must have hurt her to have to admit that Clive had turned her down – she just can't cope with failure. So the fact that she told me is a measure of her vindictiveness. She was prepared to sacrifice even her own self-esteem for the pleasure of letting me know she had preferred Clive.'

'Did you tell him you knew?'

'Yes. Her plan misfired, you see. It was intended to hurt me and to break up my friendship with Clive. And instead it reinforced the friendship, for Clive was able to talk to me freely again. And, having once admitted, to myself and to him, that the marriage had been a big mistake, I too was able to talk more freely.'

'How long did the marriage last?'

'Five years. On paper, that is. We lived together for most of that time – in a state of total indifference, at best. I had thought that our shared rationalist view of life was a good basis for marriage – having tried the opposite arrangement with such deplorable results. But I soon found out that this seemed to be the only thing we shared. I had expected something in the nature of companionship, but she had no time for anything of the sort. In fact, she was very seldom at home, and when she was she had her head in a book or was writing notes for the advancement of the cause.'

'What cause?'

'Her takeover of the business world at large, as far as I could make out. She's not a woman, she's a walking ambition. Nothing is too high for her to aim at. Even being a "mere woman" – and I hope you heard the inverted commas – isn't going to stop her.'

'I suppose it's admirable, in a way. Was that one of the things that attracted you?'

'Yes, the sheer power and drive of the woman. But I hadn't reckoned on the corresponding ruthlessness and total indifference to other people that went with this power.'

Natana was gazing thoughtfully in front of her. 'She doesn't seem to have a very amiable personality. But still, with all that energy and drive, and vision of what she might achieve – well, there's something to build on there, isn't there?'

Philip gave the girl a long look.

'Natana, are you about to suggest that I've got to learn to love her too once again?'

'That's right.' She burst out laughing. 'Every discarded wife, that's the programme ahead of you.'

'Thank God I'm not Bluebeard! But why, Natana, why do I have to learn to love this eminently unlovable woman again? I only managed to love her for a few weeks at most – and even then it wasn't real love, just a mixture of desire and vanity. Why must I learn to love her?'

'For the same reason that you must learn to love my mother again. For your own sake.'

'I'm certainly more prepared to consider it for my own

sake than for hers, I can tell you that. But it's a tall order. Love her! I can hardly even begin to consider forgiving her.'

'My father had a saying about forgiveness that has always stuck in my mind. Only a saint can afford not to forgive.'

'I like it,' said Philip. 'Paradox is a very attractive way of putting things, even if it does nothing but get you up against a blank wall of contradiction.'

'Or a blank wall of truth.'

'Hmn! Don't know about that. But then, you could hardly expect a rationalist like me to take paradox seriously, could you?'

Natana just smiled and shook her head.

'Anyway,' Philip went on, 'the point at issue, as I understand it, is that I've to learn to love both of my previous wives. Both at once, or one after another? And if so, in what order?'

'I know you're just having a quiet little laugh at me, but I'll answer your questions as if you had posed them in good faith. I think I'd take them separately, and in chronological order. And now I must get back to my hotel. I'm sure it's very late.'

'Twelve-thirty, to be exact. You can't possibly go out into the wilds of London at this time of night. You'd better stay here.'

But Natana insisted on going back to the hotel, and Philip set off with her, refusing to let her go about alone at that time of night.

'We can walk,' said the girl. 'It's not far. I deliberately chose a hotel near your flat. I had a feeling I might be making the journey several times.'

They spoke little. Philip was annoyed because she had refused to spend the night in his flat. Did she think he was going to rape her? Then it struck him that instead of rape he might perhaps have tried his hand at a little gentle seduction, and felt annoyed at himself.

Natana was aware of his grumpy state, and kept silent. Suddenly she stopped and said, 'It's here.' They were standing in front of a large building with revolving doors at the top of a few steps. 'See you tomorrow – if that's all right, that is?'

'Of course it is.'

Natana turned as if to go, then swung round again, stood on tiptoe and gave him a light peck on the cheek. Before he could even think of responding she turned again and ran lightly up the steps. Someone had just come out, and the revolving doors were still moving. With a quick, graceful movement Natana slipped into a rapidly decreasing space and disappeared.

Philip stood on the pavement watching the movement of the door, half hoping that Natana would come out again at the other side. Then he raised his hand to his face and laid his fingers on the cheek where Natana's lips had rested so briefly. He gave a great sigh and then turned to go home. But he knew he was too restless to sleep, and spent a long time wandering about the empty streets. Mooning about like a love-sick calf, he told himself. But even this attempt at realism wasn't enough to destroy the magic.

The following morning he found it extremely hard to concentrate on his work, and was thankful when it was time to go and meet Clive for lunch.

'Well? What did you think of her?' he asked.

Irritatingly, Clive said, 'Who? Natana?'

'Of course.' Philip nearly snapped at him.

'Quite a girl!'

'Is that all you have to say?'

'If you want me to be more explicit, I'm willing to admit

that she's extremely attractive, intelligent and original. That more like the thing?'

Philip nodded.

'Are you seeing her again?'

'She's coming round tonight.'

'Might I ask what for? I thought her mission was to hand over the book and see that you read it.'

'*And*, as it appears, she also considers herself committed to making sure that I react appropriately.'

'In what way?'

'By learning to love Elise again. That is the task she has set me.'

'But Elise is dead.'

'That's what I said too. But it seems that this doesn't count. It's not for her sake, but for mine, that I must learn to love her again.' As he tried to explain Natana's point of view Philip suddenly found himself more in sympathy with it than he would have thought possible. 'You see, by cutting myself off from this part of my life I've damaged myself. It's made me, well, almost desiccated. So you see, she's probably right. Perhaps the best thing I could do is learn to love Elise again.'

'Instead of which . . . oh, never mind.' Clive was about to say that Philip seemed to be making a pretty good job of loving the daughter instead. Then he decided that the question of loving Elise again was worth pursuing.

'And is this what you intend to do?'

'I'll try. But I just don't know where to begin. The whole thing seems a bit, well, bizarre.'

Clive was staring out of the window, looking as if his thoughts were miles away. He was having a struggle with his feelings, wanting to keep his secret to himself, yet convinced that he ought to do his best to help his friend.

'You could try writing,' he said at last. 'Writing letters.'

'To Elise?'

'Yes. It helps. You know they don't get there, even if you write "Please forward" on the envelope. Sometimes I've even written "Please, *please* forward"; but there's no divine postal service to see that it gets there. All the same, the writing – I mean, the mere act of writing the letter – helps. It keeps all sorts of things alive.'

Philip was silent for a while. Then he said, 'Are you still writing to her?'

'I've got a whole cupboard full of letters. But, to get back to the question in hand, I've no doubt you can do something towards getting closer to Elise. What I'm a bit worried about is just how close you're going to get to her daughter in the process.'

Philip thought of the butterfly kiss he had received the previous night, and of how completely immersed in the thought of Natana he had become during the past few days, and could find nothing to say in the way of denial.

'You think I'm in danger of falling in love with the girl?'

'I think you're in danger of making a fool of yourself. Can't you see how hideously unsuitable it is?'

'Because I'm old enough to be her father? I know there's this gap, but she's so mature that age doesn't seem to come into it. All right, all right, I know what you're going to say. You're going to point out how immature I am. But can't you see this narrows the gap even further?'

'I can't see that immaturity can be considered a recommendation, in any context whatever. But there's a much worse aspect to the thing than the mere age gap. Don't you see that it's an impossible relationship? After all, she is Elise's daughter. I mean, it's almost incestuous!'

At this point one of Clive's colleagues came up to consult him about a forthcoming appointment, and Philip was left to his own devices for a moment. The suggestion of incest had given him a nasty jolt. His immediate reaction was to reject the idea completely. Clive was allowing his sensibility to run away with him. There was, in reality, no relationship. The fact that her mother had once been his wife had nothing to do with it. And then he suddenly thought of something that seemed to shift the whole thing from the realms of metaphor to those of sheer reality, or at least possibility. Natana had told him that she was nearly twenty, when they had first met. She had since referred to her birthday, which, like his own, was early in June. Feverishly he started counting months.

By the time Clive's colleague had left him Philip had come to the conclusion that Natana must have been conceived just about the time that Elise left him. He would probably never know whether she was in fact his daughter or Miquel's. It might simply be that Elise and the Spanish painter had become lovers while she was still in London. It would help to explain the mystery of why she had gone off to join a man they had all assumed she had barely met. On the other hand . . .

Clive found Philip in a very absent frame of mind for the rest of the lunch. He wondered whether he had offended him with his outspoken words. But as they parted Philip brought himself sufficiently back into the present to say, 'I'm glad you told me about those letters,' and Clive decided that he had just been so silent because he was pondering the possibility of beginning a one-sided correspondence with Elise. Or perhaps simply the reference to Myra had brought back too many memories of their happy days together before things started to go wrong.

If concentration had been difficult in the morning, Philip now found it quite beyond his powers. All he could think of was the fact that Natana might just possibly be his daughter, and that he must on no account see her again. By now he had no illusions as to the nature of the feeling she inspired in him. There was admiration, a joyful appreciation of her originality and independence of mind, an ever-increasing willingness to begin seeing the world in the infinitely creative and satisfying way in which she saw it – and there was also a strong element of what he could only classify as sheer, carnal lust. His suggestion that she spend the night in his flat had sprung, he saw it now, as much from a hope that she might share his bed, as from a desire to protect her from the perils of midnight in London.

Halfway through the afternoon he gave up the attempt at getting any work done and went home. He took out some paper and began writing a note.

> Dear Natana,
>
> We must never meet again. I know that sounds melodramatic, but it's true. I can't even give you any sort of explanation. Our relationship began with a mystery, of your making – a tantalising, joyful, innocent mystery. And it ends with a dark and sinister question, which the Gods have thrown at us and which no man can answer.
>
> I shall try to learn to love your mother again, since this is what you wish. And that is all I can do for you.

He signed the note, put it into an envelope with her name on it, pinned it on to the door, and left the house. He had no idea where he was going. It was just a question of making sure he was away when Natana came.

After walking for an hour or two he could no longer tell what part of London he was in. He seemed to have gravitated towards the very heart of squalor. It wasn't simply a slum, it was a whole succession of slums, linked together by streets filled with derelict factories and abandoned shops. Even in the more inhabited areas some of the shops were so filthy, tattered and ill-lit that it was difficult to tell whether they were still supposed to be carrying on their trade. There were few people about, and those he saw bore the marks of chronic unemployment and deprivation. The women were all either prostitutes or misshapen, beaten-down old jades, worn out with want and overwork. The men hung about idly, sometimes talking to each other in small groups, sometimes standing alone at a street corner, talking to themselves.

Philip saw all this, and it added to his depression. But he only saw it as a backcloth to his own internal drama. It didn't occur to him to try to get out of this blighted area and get back to a more familiar, less disturbing landscape. These grim streets matched his own interior landscape too well. Their filth seemed to correspond with what he felt inside.

For his distress didn't stem merely from the fact that this girl who had taken him over so completely might in fact be his own daughter. There was no way he could prove the contrary, and that made things even worse. But the bitterest element in the whole thing consisted of his own reaction to the discovery. While a part of him drew back in horror and disgust at the thought of how near he had come to seducing his own daughter, another part of him obstinately kept on thinking of Natana's charms, and refused to stop imagining scenes of carnal delight between the two of them.

In the middle of what must have been meant as some sort of play area, surrounded by decomposing tower blocks, he sat down on a rickety bench. It had occurred to him that the thing to do was to think the matter out calmly and unemotionally, and he wanted to have all his energy available for the task.

Right, he said to himself. Natana is possibly your daughter. There's no way you can either prove or disprove that possibility. So let's assume she isn't. In that case there's no reason on earth why we shouldn't have whatever relationship we choose to have. Clive was simply being prudish in suggesting there was anything improper about it. The fact that her mother was once my wife has nothing to do with it, all the more so since Elise is now dead, so there's no question of a possible resumption of our marriage. And anyway, if that was what Elise wanted, she could have contacted me any time during the past five years, since Natana's father died. Please note, I say Natana's father, for we are working on the assumption that this is the case. Natana herself seems to have no doubt in the matter. So, if Natana is that man's daughter, there is absolutely nothing to prevent anything at all between us.

If, however, Natana is my daughter, a fact we can never know for certain, then what is the position? Society shakes its head in horror, and condemns me as an incestuous monster. But where, after all, is the evil in incest? It is, in fact, far more common than society is prepared to admit. And what harm does it do? None whatever, provided there are no children to suffer from an unwise selection of genes. If there are no children from the union, the only possible harm done is that which the condemnation of society brings. And if Natana were to know nothing of the possible incestuous relationship, she would have no cause to suffer. As for me . . .

Could I bear this burden alone?

He came to the conclusion that he could, for the sake of possessing Natana. And then the demons took over. He sat there, miles from his actual surroundings, quite unaware of what was going on about him, lost in a bitter and exquisite dream of making love to Natana. And Natana in bed was every bit as unpredictable and unselfconscious and spontaneous as Natana sitting demurely at table sharing a meal with him.

He was roused from his mental orgy by the gradual realization that there was a voice screaming somewhere near him. The noise seemed to be coming from the ground floor of the tower block against which his bench was placed. It was a long, steady, wailing sort of a howl, and it came at regular intervals, with a pause of about ten seconds between each scream.

'That's her off again,' said a voice, and he noticed to his surprise that there was a man sitting beside him on the bench. He hadn't seen him arrive, and had no idea how long he had been there. The stranger looked as down-at-heel as all the other people he had seen in the area.

'Who's off again?' asked Philip, deeply disturbed by this almost inhuman wailing.

'Doreen. Goes off like this at regular intervals, she does.'

'But why? What's the matter with her?'

His companion gave him an almost contemptuous glance. 'You lot wouldn't know, would you? Drugs, that's what it is.'

'But can't anyone do anything about it?'

'I expect someone's phoned the ambulance. They'll come – when it suits them.'

Philip felt utterly shattered by the sound. Each scream seemed to go right through his body, shaking him, jangling him. It seemed to produce an electric shock deep inside him, leaving him distraught and waiting for the next scream with the most intense apprehension.

He stood up.

'Think I'll move on,' he said.

'Not waiting to see the fun?'

'Fun?'

'When the ambulance comes. Puts up quite a fight, she does.'

'No thanks.'

He moved off, feeling some relief as the screams gradually diminished in volume.

He headed away from the tower blocks, back to the no-man's-land of derelict factories and warehouses. After a while he came to what looked like a disused level crossing, with rails leading into a tunnel. The place looked so grim and forbidding that in his disturbed state he was attracted to it. He walked along the track so far into the tunnel that he could see nothing unless he turned back and looked at the light behind him. He stood still, and soon his eyes became accustomed to the gloom, and he was able to make out a large stone lying on the ground near the wall of the tunnel. He sat down, leaned back and closed his eyes. And immediately the sweet and powerful daydream came back to him again, and he was lying in bed with Natana in his arms, and he could feel her warmth in every pore of his body, and the whole world seemed to be dancing to the rhythm of their lovemaking.

This time he was roused by a distant, threatening rumble which seemed to be getting rapidly nearer and nearer. Perhaps the line wasn't out of use after all, perhaps this was a train advancing towards him! For a moment panic seized him, and he started to stumble towards the opening he had come through. But the noise was growing rapidly louder. The train seemed to be approaching at such a pace that he knew he could never reach the entrance in time. Perhaps, he thought, this is the solution. He hadn't intended to court death. But if that was what lay in store for him, well and good. He really had nothing to live for.

The thunder increased, rolled towards him with sickening speed, and he leaned against the wall of the tunnel, closed his eyes, held his breath. And suddenly he realized that the thunder was receding. Soon the noise had disappeared, and no train had come through the tunnel.

Philip staggered towards the entrance, wondering whether he had been suffering from a hallucination of some sort, brought on by his overwrought state. But when he got out into the street and looked about him he saw that an elevated railway crossed the disused line he was on just above the tunnel. The sound he had heard had indeed been a train, but it had passed above him.

This experience left him feeling weak and shaky. He turned into a sleazy-looking pub and asked for some food and a pint of beer.

'Food? What sort of food?'

'Anything, anything.' At that precise moment he simply couldn't remember the name of anything edible. The man turned away with a shrug and a moment later presented him with a couple of cheese sandwiches.

'This do?'

'Yes, fine.'

Thinking about it later, Philip was never able to determine whether the sandwiches had been good or not, and whether the beer had been acceptable. He had eaten and he had drunk, and that was all he knew. Whatever its quality, the food gave him enough sustenance to resume his wandering. It was long after nightfall before he found himself in a recognizable part of the town. He was still a long way from his flat, and almost too tired to walk. He stood on the pavement for a long time, hoping for a cruising taxi. At last one appeared and he flagged it down and practically fell into it.

'Been having quite a night of it, eh, mate?'

All Philip could manage as he sank down onto the back seat was a groan. The driver chuckled and shook his head, with a mixture of sympathy and envy.

'Where to, then?'

Philip managed to remember his address and articulate it

clearly enough for the man to understand. By the time they got there he had recovered sufficiently to struggle out of the taxi and into the lift.

As he stepped out to the landing he noticed the figure standing beside his door, leaning against the wall in an attitude of complete exhaustion. They stared at each other in silence. Then Philip opened the door and stood aside to let her in.

11

Neither said a word till they had sat down opposite each other. Then Natana spoke. She waved a piece of paper at him that he recognized as his note.

'What's the meaning of this?' she asked. He was shocked by the sound of her voice. Its usual warmth and vibrancy had gone, and it sounded dead and flat. And now he noticed how tired and drawn she looked.

'You look terrible,' he said, forgetting all about her question.

'So do you,' she retorted. 'But I want to know what this is all about.' And once again she waved the note.

Suddenly he realized that he had been deliberately deceiving himself with his pious hope that Natana might never guess the possible relationship between them. How could an intelligent girl like her fail to realize it?

'Can't you guess?'

Natana shook her head in bewilderment. Then she asked, 'It wasn't . . . it wouldn't be because of . . . of that kiss?'

'Good heavens, no! Of course not!'

'Then I simply can't imagine what it's all about.'

'Just a simple matter of arithmetic.'

Natana looked even more mystified. Again she shook her head.

'I don't know what on earth you mean. My arithmetic isn't very good, anyway.'

'I think it should rise to counting up to twenty years and nine months.'

Natana's face was a picture of astonishment. Then suddenly she blushed crimson.

'Oh, my God!' she whispered, and said nothing else for a while.

At last she spoke, in a small, uncertain voice.

'I see I've done something terrible. I'm sorry, it never occurred to me it could lead to such a misunderstanding. You see, I just wanted to sound grown-up. It seemed important, in the circumstances – and, anyway, one always does,' she admitted. 'And so I said I was nearly twenty. But in fact that was a bit of an exaggeration. Actually, I'll be nineteen next month. So what you were thinking of simply doesn't apply.'

Philip stared at her in a mixture of relief and outrage. He thought of the specious arguments and forbidden fantasies in which he had indulged, all triggered off by the wrong information the girl had given him, and the relief he felt was offset by the knowledge that from now on he was going to have to face the fact that he was capable of wandering into these dark areas of the soul, just as he had wandered into those slums that the acceptable part of the city knew nothing about. From now on he was going to have to live with the slums of his own mind.

After a moment of silence, while he thought over the new situation, he said:

'Natana, I could wring your neck.'

'I know. It was all my doing. But how could I have guessed? When did it first occur to you? That I might be your daughter, I mean?'

'When I was having lunch with Clive. Something he said made me suddenly remember you had said you were nearly twenty, and the rest seemed to follow.'

Natana gave a great sigh. 'I'm so glad. So glad it wasn't till then. I'd have hated to think that this was on your mind all along. And I'm sorry, really sorry. I should have remembered the saying about the tangled web, shouldn't I? And actually, in case you have any lingering doubts left, I think I can prove conclusively that I'm my father's daughter. I brought along some photos of my mother and, at the last minute, I slipped this one in as well. I just thought you might like to see what my father looked like, little knowing how relevant this might be.'

From her handbag she had taken out a bunch of photos, and she handed one over to Philip. It was a snap of Miquel standing beside one of his canvases. The likeness between father and daughter was startling. Philip gazed at it for a long time.

'Proof positive,' he said. 'I reckon any court of law would take that as evidence. He looks a nice man. Which follows, of course, if he was so like you.'

'You're not angry with me any more, then?'

'No, Natana, I'm not angry with you. I'm angry with myself – horrified, in fact. But that's got nothing to do with you, or with your innocent lie.'

'My innocent lie that had such devastating repercussions. Oh, Philip, if you knew what a time I've had, waiting there outside your door, not knowing what on earth was the matter!'

Natana had put Miquel's photo back into her bag, and she sat with the others in her hand. Hesitantly she said, 'Would you like to see some photos of my mother?'

Philip thought of Clive and his letters to Myra, and it struck him that there was much to be said for not shutting oneself off from one's dead. He leaned forward and held out his hand. Natana stretched forward too and handed him the bundle of photos.

Elise had preserved her beauty in middle-age. Even in the last snaps before her sudden death there were few signs of ageing. A few fine wrinkles round the eyes, a softer, mellower line to the curves of her jawbone. But it was still the same delicate, ethereal face, with its big, clear eyes that seemed to be looking into another world.

Philip gazed in silence for so long that at length Natana spoke.

'Lovely, wasn't she?'

Philip nodded. He tried to say something and burst into a storm of uncontrollable weeping. He had no idea how long it lasted. It seemed to him that he had the tears of more than twenty years to release. When at last the storm was over he looked up, trying to take stock of where he was. He saw that the photos had fallen from his hands and lay scattered on the floor. Natana had stretched out on the couch and was sleeping peacefully.

He went over and stood beside her, watching her relaxed features, her even, quiet breathing. In her total abandonment and trust she looked like a sleeping child. Quietly he walked through to the guest room and took the quilt off the bed. Then he carried it back to the sitting room and laid it tenderly over Natana. She gave a little sigh, then resumed her gentle, even breathing. He stood looking at her for a long time, thinking over the events and emotions of the past few days. He would have liked to spend all night watching her, but his exhaustion overcame him, and he went to bed. Almost at once he was sleeping as peacefully as Natana.

The following morning he got up at his usual time and went through to the sitting room. The first thing he saw was the collection of photos neatly arranged on the mantelpiece. Then he looked down at the couch.

Natana was not there, but the quilt had been folded and laid on a chair nearby.

'Natana!'

'I'm here.' Natana had heard the panic in his voice, and came out of the kitchen to reassure him. 'Just making breakfast. Are you hungry?'

'Probably. I haven't had time to find out yet. Are you?'

'I'm always hungry when I get up. Did you sleep well?'

'Divinely. But I should be asking you. You're the guest. And you didn't even have a proper bed to sleep on. What hospitality!'

'I slept beautifully. Do I look like I've had a bad night?'

Philip shook his head. 'You don't even look like someone who's slept all night in the same clothes. How do you do it?'

'Well, it can't be practice. I've never done anything of the sort before. I'm very grateful to you. Another first.'

'Another first?'

'I collect firsts. This was my first time of sleeping with all my clothes on.'

'That's youth. Able to exult in an uncomfortable experience.'

'But it wasn't uncomfortable. I slept like an angel.'

'You're right. That's what you looked like.'

'Talking of angels, would you like to keep some of those photos of my mother?'

'Of course I would.'

She looked up and smiled:

'We've come a long way in a few days, haven't we? I don't think you'd have thanked me for one of my mother's photos at the beginning of the week, would you?'

'No, perhaps not. But since I've been given the job of learning to love her again . . . '

'You might as well have some of the props, is that it?'

'Natana, tell me what you thought, when you got my note. All those hours standing waiting.'

'I didn't stand all the time. Every so often I sat down on the stairs, till it got too hard or till I heard someone coming. Then I would leap up and pretend I had just rung. It was a bit awkward, really. Especially when the lady from the door opposite came and told me she thought you must be out. I nearly said yes, I knew you were out, that I had a note to prove it. And then it struck me that she might think that distinctly erratic behaviour and send for the police who would have me up for loitering, which was exactly what I was doing, so I meekly said yes, it did look as if you were out, and I pretended to go away. But I stopped in the entrance hall and sneaked back up again.'

'You still haven't told me what you thought, all those hours.'

'I'll tell you if you promise to tell me what you were doing and thinking all that time.'

'All right, I promise. You start. After all, I asked first.'

'The first thing I thought when I read your note was that I'd gone mad. Then I thought that perhaps you had. I simply couldn't imagine what dark and sinister question the Gods could have thrown at us that meant that we must never meet again. That, I think, was the worst bit of the whole experience, the fact that I simply couldn't make any sense of the thing. I simply couldn't see what even the most evil and arbitrary of Gods could have thought up to keep us apart in this melodramatic way. The only thing that sustained me was the hope that there must have been some terrible misunderstanding between us, but I simply couldn't think what it might be. I wondered whether you were annoyed because I had refused to spend the previous night here. I blamed myself for being prudish and schoolgirlish – and the event has shown how wrong I was to refuse. Here I am at breakfast with you, having spent the night in your flat in unmolested peace and quiet.'

At this point Philip found himself wondering whether things would have been quite so quiet and peaceful if she had stayed that night when he asked her to, before the bombshell of their possible relationship had burst.

'And then my thoughts veered off in the opposite direction,' Natana continued. 'I remembered the kiss I had given you and wondered whether you'd been offended at that. But it was only a light peck on the cheek, wasn't it?'

'I might have been offended because that's all it was.'

'But you weren't, were you?'

'No. I was delighted with it. It was lovely.'

'I thought so too. So, you see, I simply didn't know what to think. I wondered whether you'd had some sort of brainstorm and were desperately needing help somewhere. Perhaps you were even lying unconscious in the house. Time and again I was on the point of going to the police and asking them to force their way in. But I didn't know what sort of reception I'd get. I knew they'd ask all sorts of questions that I couldn't answer, for I really don't know you all that well. And they'd want to know what I was doing here anyway, and I know your policemen are wonderful, but what would they make of the fact that I'd come here on behalf of my mother to try to get you to love her again, especially since I'd probably have had to admit that she's dead?

'In the end I began to wonder what sort of a person I really was. I'm not greatly given to self-analysis, and suddenly it seemed to me that I really knew nothing about myself. I wondered whether I had been saying terrible things or behaving in an utterly unacceptable way. And then I thought about what you had said about the Gods and their sinister question, and I just couldn't make sense of any of it. And I was so tired, oh, so tired!'

'But you didn't think of going back to your hotel?'

'No, not till I'd seen you. And I wanted to be there when you came back – assuming you were out in the first place. I was afraid that if I came back in the morning and you were at home you wouldn't let me in. So I just waited and waited, and in the end you came back, and it's all right now, isn't it?'

'Yes, it's all right. Thanks to your endurance. Anyone else might have given up and gone away, and we'd never have got things straightened out.'

After a silence Natana said, 'What were you up to all that time? Where were you?'

'I was in hell.'

'Metaphorically?'

'And literally, just about.'

'Tell me.'

'Are you sure you want a conducted tour of hell?'

'It's part of the bargain. I've already given you a description of my little bit of it.'

Philip wasn't at all keen on the idea of giving Natana any insight into the sort of psychological hell he had been through. How could he possibly tell this girl about the illicit fantasies he had indulged in with her as an unsuspecting accomplice? That part at least he must suppress. But how much should he tell her of the fear and misery which his suspicions about her parentage had aroused? He would start off by telling her about the objective hell he had visited. The rest might follow.

'Don't ask me where I was, for I don't know. There are areas in London I didn't even know existed. Streets of disused factories and empty warehouses. Streets and streets that look as if they should have been pulled down years ago. And the tragedy is that most of them probably were. Many of these slums I was wandering through are recent. You can tell from the high-rise architecture. Built within the past thirty years, and converted into slums within a year or two of construction, from the look of things.'

'And the people?'

'The people have been made to fit their surroundings – or the other way round, I don't know. Even if I'd been feeling perfectly happy in the first place I'd have come away deeply disturbed by what I saw. The place has been vandalised, and the people look as if they have too. And I don't know whose fault it is.'

He went on to tell her some of the sights he had seen, some of the sounds he had heard, including the rhythmical screaming of the drug addict. 'It was the most horrifying sound I've ever heard. I thought I'd hear it for the rest of my life. And I suspect I will, though at intervals.'

'You didn't hear it in your dreams last night?'

'I had no dreams last night. I just slept and slept.'

'Me too. Funny, isn't it? It was almost worth going through all that misery, for the sake of the wonderful relief that followed. I suppose that's why we both slept so well.'

'Perhaps. But I don't think I'd recommend this sort of nightmare as a general cure for insomnia.'

He went on to tell her of his experience in the tunnel, and his belief that the approaching train was on the very line he was on. He spoke of his conviction that death was imminent.

'Were you afraid?'

'Yes, I think I was afraid. But in a way I didn't really mind. Life seemed too hideous and horrible to want to hang on to it.'

'Life in general, after what you had seen of those slums, or your own life in particular?'

'Both. None of these people I had seen seemed to have anything worth living for. And I felt that I hadn't either, and that the world wouldn't be much the worse for losing me.'

'Why did you feel the world would be none the worse for losing you?'

'Because of my sense of guilt.' Now, he thought. Now she's going to ask me what I felt guilty about, and I'm going to have to tell her.

But Natana didn't ask the expected question. Instead she said, 'Well? What happened? I know the train didn't kill you, but I want to know why.'

'Because it wasn't in my tunnel. It crossed it on a higher level. But the noise!'

'Another unforgettable noise?'

'Yes, but less so. I think I'll be able to forget this one. After all, it ended in anticlimax. I'd simply got my facts wrong. The noise was there, but it posed no threat. It meant nothing. The danger was imaginary.'

'Whereas the screaming was for real.'

'Yes. No question of misunderstanding there. No *deus ex machina* can explain that one away. Ever.'

There was a silence and then Natana asked, 'How did you get back here?'

'I wandered about in that desolate no man's land till at last I came to something more like the London I'm used to, and eventually I managed to flag down a cruising taxi. I was in such a state of exhaustion and misery that the driver thought I'd been out celebrating. I think he was envious.'

Natana sat looking thoughtful for a time. When she spoke it was to ask him whether he was going out to work that morning.

'Yes, I'd better. I've simply not concentrated on anything this week, and things are piling up. Will you be here when I come back?'

'Yes, if you give me a key. I've things to do. One of them is arrange about going back home. Tomorrow, I think.'

'Oh, Natana! So soon?'

'Yes, I think I must. Besides, there's a young man in Perpignan . . . '

'To whom you are committed?'

'No, but I'd like to be. Only he's not so keen.'

'He must be mad.'

'Thank you. That restores my self-esteem a little. Perhaps he'll like me better after all my foreign travel.'

Natana had exaggerated a little. She cared for Pierre, perhaps a little more than he cared for her, but she wasn't at all sure that she really wanted to be committed to him. Still, it was a useful excuse for getting away. She had realised the cause of Philip's distress when he thought she might be his daughter, and felt that a prolonged stay in London might just lead to complications for both of them. She liked Philip, she liked him immensely, and wished she could do more for him. But perhaps the best thing she could do for him was put a few hundred miles between them. And exaggerating her feelings for Pierre could do nothing but good, in the present circumstances. A little inaccuracy can be quite a useful thing. Then she thought of the crisis that her little inaccuracy about her age had triggered off, and made a mental note to restrain herself in future, however useful it might be to alter the facts just a little.

The first thing Natana did after Philip had gone to work was start looking through the London telephone directory. She was amazed at the size of the thing. She had assumed that one volume would cover it. Not like dear little Perpignan, she thought, realizing it might take a lot longer than she thought. And I don't even know whether the damn woman still lives in London. Or what name to look under. She may have married again, or gone back to her maiden name. After all, it's ten years!

There were quite a few Lockes listed, but none of them with the name Davina. In the end she decided that her only hope was a Dr D M Locke, who lived in St John's Wood. She put off the visit till the afternoon, and spent the morning seeing about booking her flight. Then she went to her hotel, changed into the smartest clothes she had with her and set off.

Even Natana had to admit that this new mission was a pretty tricky one. But then, that was what she had thought about tackling Philip, and things seemed to be turning out remarkably well. There had been difficulties, of course, and last night she would have said that the situation was utterly hopeless, that she had achieved nothing and possibly done immeasurable harm with her well-intentioned interference. But still, all things considered, she was convinced that Philip was in a much more accessible state of mind than at first, and she felt pretty sure that, even if he would never accept the point of view that she and her mother shared, he was at least less hostile to it and to her mother's memory.

With that achievement behind her, she felt ready to tackle this other task she had set herself. For if she could leave, having not only softened Philip's attitude to his first wife, but also done something towards a reconciliation with the second wife, she could feel she had really succeeded in her mission. Her mother would then have cause to be proud of her daughter.

She was realistic enough to appreciate that her youth and attractive appearance, which had played some part in the winning over of Philip, might prove to be a minus rather than a plus in the present undertaking. Still, she knew she got on well with people in general. And if what she had heard of this woman was hardly prepossessing, well, what she had known of Philip before meeting him had not shown him in a particularly favourable light. She had tried to meet Philip with an unprejudiced mind, and it had paid dividends.

No doubt a similar approach on this occasion would prove equally fruitful.

Anyway, she told herself, if I get nowhere with this woman I don't need to feel I've failed utterly. What I'm doing now is quite outside my original remit. Philip said in his note – his terrible note! – that he would do his best to try to learn to love my mother again, and that's all I really set out to do. She resolved that they would speak more about her in the evening. And he had the photographs. How could any man look on that beautiful face and not be filled with love? Yes, she felt sure that by the time she left she would have effected a reconciliation between Philip and his first wife. And, who knows, perhaps the second one too?

12

'I really don't know why I married him. I suppose he just swept me off my feet. Very insistent, he was. And I must admit, he really was very presentable, and most intelligent, of course. And he had this friend, and he was all right too, and also very keen on me, and the three of us used to go about together. Perhaps I should have married the other one.'

'Or both, perhaps?' suggested Basil helpfully.

'Why not?' said Davina. Then she gave a little laugh. 'Much too conventional, those two, for anything of the sort.'

'You don't see them in a *ménage à trois*?'

'Not really.' Davina was never very comfortable with French, and she suspected that Basil had guessed as much. 'Anyway, that's all ancient history,' she went on. 'I'm really only interested in the present.'

'Not the future?' There was a touch of malice in Basil's question. 'Given up worrying about your empire-building?'

Davina was about to wither him with a look, then reminded herself that this man was actually the younger brother of an earl. She gave a shrug. 'I prefer not to think about the future at the moment. I'll fight another day.'

'Which implies that at present you have run away.'

'We'll see about that. That fat pig of an Adrian may think

he's won this round, but that's not the end of the game. Not by a long chalk. We'll see who laughs last.'

'You're being very proverbial today, my dear.'

Davina was having some difficulty in restraining her resentment. She had just lost a battle at work, and was trying to persuade herself that in her private life at least all was going well. She could hardly say it was going according to plan, because being the mistress of an aristocratic twit, as she referred to Basil in the privacy of her mind, was in fact a higher rank than she had hoped to attain. He was, of course, penniless, and she fully understood that one of her attractions was the fact that she could afford to keep this fashionable lapdog. And even if her money was the only attraction, so what? Davina had never had any belief in the value of human relationships, or in the sincerity of any protestations of love or loyalty. The fact that Basil made no attempt at convincing her of the depths of his feelings for her was in a way irritating, in that it revealed an unspoken contempt; but it was also refreshing not to have to deal with a lot of cant. And she knew she could get rid of him the moment she wanted to. All she had to do was cut off his allowance.

If her love-life, as it amused her to call it, seemed to be prospering at this moment, the real business of her life was proving rather less tractable. For years she had ridden on the crest of the wave, with promotion after promotion to give her the heady conviction that nothing could stop her from reaching the top. She had set her sights on the directorship of the large company she was with – as the current aim. After that she knew herself well enough to realize that she would then find some even higher achievement to target. But over the last few years progress had become increasingly slow. In fact, it looked as if her present efforts were doomed to failure. She had only two to go, as she put it, only two more people above her to topple, but for a long time she seemed to have made no progress.

And then, only a few weeks ago, in a boardroom reshuffle, she had seen her opportunity and taken it. She could have sworn she had enough people on her side to carry it off. And the worst of it, the most infuriating thing of it all, was that Adrian, for whose consolation, or, more accurately, for whose mortification, she had thought up a number of suitable words of commiseration, such as 'luck of the draw', 'you can't win them all' and 'every dog must have his day'; this same Adrian had had the cheek to throw a few remarkably similar observations in her direction, along with a piece of friendly advice.

'Your problem, Davina,' he had said with a benign expression, 'is that you've just not given enough thought to the public-relations bit. Pity, really, when one thinks of the immense amount of effort you've expended. You're so clued up in all other respects – you've got the technical know-how, and the business experience, you've got the vision and the ambition. And then you let it all slip through your fingers because you underestimate the human element. PR, Davina, PR, that's the secret of success. You can get so far without it, but if you're really aiming for the top . . . ' And Adrian had shaken his head with the most irritating smugness.

Right, my man, thought Davina. You're aiming for the top too, and you're one step ahead of me at present, but we'll see who gets there first. Aloud she merely said, 'Thanks for the advice. But I wouldn't go around dishing out too many useful hints to possible rivals. You might regret it some day. One can be too successful.'

Adrian chuckled. 'I'm not too worried. I don't see you making a success of the public-relations thing even if you tried.'

'Why not?'

'You're too bloody self-centred! You don't really believe that other people exist. And they notice, you know. They notice.'

'You can't get to the top without being hard as nails. In the end your PR amounts to nothing more than hypocrisy.'

Adrian chuckled again. 'What's in a name?'

Davina tried to brazen it out with herself. On the one hand she assured herself that she would win in the long run, PR or no PR; and at the same time she congratulated herself on her lack of hypocrisy. But deep down she knew she would have to make an important decision soon. Either she must aim straight for the top, trying to by-pass Adrian – and what glory that would be! – or else she must seek pastures new. The first option, if successful, would be deeply satisfying. On the other hand, it was an almost impossible task to set herself, and failure would leave her in a totally untenable position, not only in her own firm. These things get around, she reminded herself. Instead of toppling the present director she might very well topple herself. And if that happened her only hope of climbing back up would consist in going abroad again.

These thoughts were troubling her so deeply at that moment that she was quite unable to enjoy the idle and malicious chatter of the loquacious Basil.

'And I find that, when people start quoting proverbs at you, there's usually a reason for it.'

'There's a reason for everything, or so they say,' she remarked tartly.

'There you go again. There's a reason for everything, she says. Proverbial again. And this particular dictum seems to argue a greater faith in the rationality of the universe than I gave you credit for.'

'In that case, it's clear that you know even less about me

than I thought you did. The one thing I believe in, wholly and unreservedly, is the necessity of cause and effect. Reasons, facts, observable and measurable phenomena – these are the only things that count.'

'Yes, Dr Locke. And to what do you attribute your limited vision? You've never told me anything about your early days. What sort of a home did you come from? Were your parents as rationally inclined as you?'

'My life began when I graduated out of university. Before that I had not begun to exist.'

'So you had no parents?'

'Exactly.'

'Good. I like that. I'm only sorry I never thought of saying the same. Not that I have anything against my parents, dear good people. I could have wished that they had given me a little more, either in the way of wealth or in the way of energy with which to acquire a little more of the former. But no, I can't really hold it against them that they didn't manage to give me enough of either. I'm sure they did their best. What I like about your way of dispensing with parents, which are usually considered so indispensable, is simply the originality of the idea. I wish I'd thought of it myself.'

Davina felt a slight improvement in spirits. To be considered original by a member of the upper classes helped to restore her emotional balance. Blow PR, she thought. It may be necessary for the plodders. I'm a cut above them.

But Basil's next observation plunged her back into her previous irritation. 'And if I had thought of it, it would of course have been infinitely more original,' he pointed out. 'For I have every reason to be proud of my parents, so negating them in this way would really have been a stroke of genius, a piece of gratuitous effrontery. Your situation necessarily prevents you from earning the full glory of the act in its highest form.'

'You know nothing whatever about my situation.'

'Precisely. And that in itself speaks volumes.'

Just then they heard the buzzer sounding in the hall. Davina didn't move.

'Aren't you going to answer?'

'No. I can't think of anyone I want to see at present.'

'I'll go. I'll go and say you're out.'

She shrugged. 'If you like.'

When Basil answered he heard Natana's voice speaking to him from downstairs. He liked the voice, with its youthful ring, and said yes, Dr Locke was at home, and would the visitor just come up.

'Who was it?'

'A charming young lady with an impossible name. I've asked her up.'

'Why, might I ask?'

'I thought both of us could do with a fresh young voice in the room.'

'She may be an old hag.'

'I've no doubt you'll be less disappointed than I shall, if that's the case. That sounds like the lift,' he said, and went to open the door.

He was distinctly pleased with what he saw.

'Do come in,' he said graciously. 'I'm afraid I didn't quite catch your name, my dear.'

'Natana Planas. Can I see Dr Locke?'

Basil ushered her into the lounge, where Davina didn't trouble to get up to greet her guest.

'This is Natana,' said Basil in tones of great satisfaction.

'Well? To what do I owe the honour?'

Natana was aware of the insolence of the tone, and found herself at a loss. She had prepared no introductory speech, relying on the inspiration of the moment. And the moment, she now found, does not always inspire.

'I thought, I mean, I wanted to have a word with you, about a private matter.' This wasn't really what she wanted to say. Not only did it sound feeble, but it seemed to exclude the friendly member of the company, leaving her alone with the markedly hostile one. She turned a troubled face to Basil.

'I'll go, if you insist,' he said. 'But it will be a blow.'

'No. Please don't go. I didn't mean that at all.'

Davina broke in. 'When you've both finished settling the matter of who I receive, and how, in my own house, perhaps we can find out what all this is about. Did you say your name was Natana?'

'Yes, that's right.'

'Who ever gave you a name like that?'

'My parents, of course.' Natana spoke almost sharply, aware of the implied criticism.

'I'm afraid our friend Dr Locke doesn't believe in parents. She assures me she never had any.'

'Oh!' exclaimed Natana, 'how sad!' Suddenly she felt less ill-disposed towards the other woman. An orphan! That would explain her difficult behaviour, both now and in the past.

Davina exchanged an amused look with Basil, more ironic than friendly on her part.

'I'm afraid I haven't made myself clear,' said Basil. 'Our friend here has merely suffered a voluntary deprivation of parents. A case of would-be auto-genesis.'

Ignoring him, Davina spoke again. 'We don't seem to be making much progress, do we? I still don't know what you're doing here. If you can't come up with something plausible pretty soon I'll be forced to the conclusion that you're simply casing the joint.'

Natana was feeling increasingly foolish, and this last expression, which she had never heard before, but which evidently was meant to be insulting, did nothing to reassure her.

'It's rather a long story.'

Here Davina sighed.

'And a rather odd one too,' Natana admitted.

'Splendid!' exclaimed Basil. 'Just what we need to brighten up our tedious little lives. A long, odd story. Splendid!'

He knew he was incurring Davina's displeasure at every word, but felt he could afford to do so at present. The liaison with a member of the aristocracy was still too recent a thing for Davina to be prepared to give it up just yet. Basil was familiar with this type of situation, and knew just how much any given patron would stand. In this case he was sure he was nowhere near breaking point yet, especially after the failure of Davina's bid for power. No, Davina was good for quite a few months yet.

'I've come, I suppose, really, on behalf of my mother, who was hoping for a reconciliation with her first husband.'

'Not your father?' inquired Basil.

'I belong to the second marriage.'

'And what does your father have to say about this proposed reconciliation?' Davina was beginning to find some interest in the conversation.

'Nothing, now. He's dead.'

'I see,' said Davina. 'So, having lost her second husband, your mother now wants to go back to the first?'

'Not exactly. She actually wanted this reconciliation some time before my father died, and he encouraged her.'

'Really?' Davina sounded amused. 'Wanted rid of her, I take it?'

'No, nothing like that. He just wanted her to be happy.'

'Generous man!' exclaimed Basil.

Natana couldn't quite make out whether this was meant ironically or not.

'He was the most generous of men,' she asserted.

Davina agreed. 'So it seems. And now he's dead it appears your mother will have to make do with only one husband. All I can say is, if he's anything like my first – and probably last – husband, she's better off without him.'

Natana now realised that the underlying goodness that she had attributed to Davina was perhaps buried too deep to be of much practical help. She had given up hoping for a friendly, understanding conversation, and was now beginning to enjoy knowing so much more of the facts of the case than either of her companions. If at first she had contributed to their mystification by her own embarrassment and uncertainty, now she allowed herself to play a little game of cat and mouse with them.

'I'm afraid the situation isn't as simple as that. The problem is that my mother is dead too.'

Basil gave a whoop of joy. 'Magnificent! Quite a *coup de théâtre*!' He looked placidly at Davina as he uttered the words in French.

Davina said nothing, but allowed an overtly sceptical expression to appear on her face.

'So what you are seeking, I take it,' went on Basil, 'is a posthumous reconciliation?'

'Exactly. That's a very good way of putting it. And I rather think I'm going to succeed.'

Davina smiled with scornful amusement. 'You've got him softened up, have you?'

'Well, yes, if you put it that way. I think I have.'

'Really? I suppose we'd better not inquire into your methods.'

Natana blushed angrily.

'My "methods", as you call them, consisted of showing him some of her more recent photographs, and a book.'

'Not too recent, I presume. After all, your mother could hardly be a young woman. Time takes its toll.'

'There you are, you see! Going all sententious again.'

Natana ignored this interruption from Basil. 'My mother was very beautiful right up to the day she died. *She* had nothing to fear from the passage of time.' Looking at Davina she decided that she too had worn pretty well, considering she must now be in her early forties. She was still slim and athletic-looking, and the worst that could be said of her face was that it would have been the better for rather less hardness.

'And the book? Do tell us about the book,' demanded Basil. 'I'm trying to think of a suitable title for the situation. How about *Limbo Lovers*, or *Let's Try Again, Darling*?'

'The book is called *The Occult in Daily Life*.'

'And that's turned him on?'

'I think it has changed his attitude quite a lot.' Natana felt she really couldn't claim too much for the book just yet. She suspected that the breakthrough had come rather from the photos and her own intervention. In time, she hoped the book would come into its own, after she had gone.

'Right,' said Davina. 'We now have some fascinating information. What still remains to be explained is what all this has to do with me. For it was me you asked to see, if you remember.'

'Yes, I do remember, very clearly. And the connexion is that my mother's first husband was also your husband, Philip Locke.'

Davina received the news with an expressionless face. But Basil exploded into delighted exclamations.

'Splendid! And so appropriate! I mean, talk of angels! Just before you arrived Davina was telling me all about her husband and how he had simply swept her off her feet. It seems he was desperately keen.'

Davina continued to keep an utterly expressionless face. She suspected that Philip had probably told Natana enough about the marriage for the girl to realize the falsity of this version.

'Really?' Natana smiled with demure incredulity.

Davina decided it was time to take the offensive.

'As I see it, your mother commissioned you – was it a death-bed wish? – to effect a reconciliation with her first husband, who, as it happens, was also my husband, and, as I said before, hopefully my last. And when I say that, I really mean it. Nothing would persuade me to marry again. Not even this dear man here, who happens to be the brother of an earl. I point that out merely to show the depths of my aversion to the thought of marriage. And the one and only person responsible for that aversion is none other than this Philip Locke you have just mentioned. If, therefore, it was part of your mother's wish that there should be a reconciliation between him and his second wife – and I can think of no other reason for your being here, unlikely as that is – then all I can say is that you're wasting your time, as well as mine and this gentleman's.'

'Not mine, Davina! Allow me to speak for myself in this matter. I'm having a lovely time. But I really don't see why your mother should want her former husband to be reconciled to his second wife. Might there not be cause for jealousy? Especially as the second one has the unquestionable advantage of being alive, therefore rather more *sur place*, as it were.'

Natana looked a trifle uneasy. 'I must admit that wasn't really part of my commission. It just occurred to me this morning and I acted on it right away, as I tend to do. Perhaps I hadn't worked out all the implications. But I'm sure, all the same, that if I'd succeeded, Mummy would have thought it a good idea. It wasn't only my father who was generous,' she added defiantly.

'Does Philip know of your plan?' asked Davina. She very much hoped he did. For if Philip had been keen to renew their relationship it would have perhaps given some credence to the statements she had made earlier about his devotion. And she would have had that much more satisfaction in turning him down.

'No. It was entirely my own idea. If he knew I was here I think he'd kill me.' Natana saw the amusement that this statement produced in Basil, and felt gratified.

Davina was not amused. She looked coldly at Natana and said, 'You must be what's known as an inveterate do-gooder. I'm sorry to have to say that about anyone, but there's obviously no other explanation. A combination of ignorance, interference and self-confidence, that's what it amounts to. I've seen a lot of it in my time, but never quite like this. You can have the satisfaction of knowing you're the worst example I've ever come across.'

'I can have the satisfaction of having failed, now that I know what you're like.'

Natana stood up and Basil rose too, with *empressement*. But Davina beat him to the door. 'I'll see our little innocent out,' she said with such firmness that all he could do was bow and murmur, 'Delighted. And that's not just a formula.'

Natana was too flustered to be able to recognize this tribute with more than an awkward nod as she followed Davina out of the room. She would have liked to find some way of acknowledging the fact that he had been friendly, even if possibly for the wrong reasons. Besides, if he really was brother to an earl . . .

Davina opened the front door and stood beside it imperiously. 'You'd better do some growing up before you try interfering in adult lives again,' she said.

Her departing guest would dearly have loved to think up some devastating riposte, but no words came. She walked out in silence, trying to hold her head high.

She was in such a state of mental disarray that she got confused about which line she ought to be on in the underground, and found herself miles out of her way. By the time she had worked out what train she ought to take, and in which direction, the rush hour was on. She arrived at Philip's feeling depressed and incompetent, and found him already there.

'You said you'd be back when I got home,' he said accusingly.

'I'm sorry, I got lost. And you needn't snap at me.'

'I didn't snap at you.'

Natana said nothing, but gave him a reproachful look.

Philip recanted. 'I'm sorry. I suppose I did snap. It's just that I was so worried. And if this is to be your last evening here I didn't want to miss any of it.'

Natana gave him a wan smile. 'I know. It was silly of me to get lost. And then I landed in the rush hour. I don't think I'd like to live in a big city like this. It makes you feel very small, doesn't it?'

'Not once you know the place thoroughly. Or perhaps it's just that you get used to feeling small, and stop noticing. Where were you, anyway?'

Natana had left the house hoping to greet Philip with the triumphant news of a reconciliation. She hadn't got round to deciding whether she should tell him about her failed attempt, or preserve a discreet silence. But, faced with this point-blank question, she found she had no answer ready, and gazed at him in discomfiture.

'Perhaps I'd no right to ask. Forget it, if you don't want to tell me.'

'It's not that. Oh, Philip, I've just discovered how stupid I can be, and how bitchy.' And she burst into tears. As soon as she had recovered her composure she told him the whole episode.

'And I suspect she was right, when she told me I was ignorant and interfering and self-confident.'

'She was right about the last bit. You are self-confident. Delightfully so. You had to be, to take on this assignment. There are very few daughters who would have been capable of taking that on for the sake of their mother. And that's something I meant to ask you. Your mother didn't know anything about your coming to me, did she?'

'No, she meant to come herself. And it wasn't till months after she'd died that it struck me I could do it for her. But I'm sure if she'd had any warning that she was about to die, she'd have asked me. I don't know whether simply sending you the book would have done the trick, even if I'd explained who it was written by, and why.'

'No, it certainly wouldn't. It would have taken an emissary like you to convince me. After all, I'm not at all convinced by the book's arguments.'

'But you will be, perhaps, some time?'

'I think it unlikely. I admit I'm certainly less hostile, but that's as far as I can go. But that's not to say your mother didn't achieve her purpose in writing it, if it was meant to bring the two of us closer together again. It's *you* that's achieved this, and you've been able to do it because of the book.'

'Will you remember that the reason she wanted to bring you both together again was so that your life could be enriched with a less materialistic and cerebral system of beliefs? That was really what it was all about. And I should have remembered that when I set out to bring you and that woman together. It could have done you nothing but harm. She's a bitch of the highest order. And the worst of it was that I found her bringing out all the latent bitchiness in me. I said some horrible things, and enjoyed saying them.'

Philip laughed. 'I'm sure she deserved them. But tell me about this earl's brother. Do you think this is true?'

'He looked and sounded effete enough. And he didn't deny it. It may not be true, but I think she thinks it is. She sounded so triumphant when she mentioned that detail. He was quite nice, really, but pretty seedy-looking. If he really is an aristocrat he's obviously not exactly an ornament to the family.'

Later they reverted to the subject of Elise, and of Philip's projected attempt to learn to love her again.

'Have you any idea of how you're going to set about it?'

'Yes. There are the photos. And then, I'm going to write to her.'

'Oh, Philip, what a wonderful idea! So that means you really do believe in some form of communication?'

He shook his head. 'No. Not yet, anyway,' he added, seeing her disappointment. 'I got the idea from Clive. He told me the other day that he's been writing to Myra ever since her death more than twenty years ago. Now, it's not that he believes that there's any Myra left, in any form, to receive the letters. Or if he does he can't admit it, not even to himself. It just helps to make it more bearable for him. And even if I can get no further than that, simply writing for what it's doing for me, helping me to . . . to clarify the past, if you like, then that in itself is what your mother was hoping for, wasn't it?'

'I'm so glad, Philip. So glad for you – and for her,' she added almost defiantly.

Natana refused to spend the night at Philip's flat, and he

didn't urge her. Both were happy about their relationship as it was, and both felt the danger of too close a contact. Although it was their last evening together Philip accompanied her to her hotel at a reasonably early hour, promising to take her to the airport the following day. Once again she gave him a fleeting goodnight kiss. This time Philip saw to it that it didn't throw him off balance as on the first occasion. I think it was partly the element of surprise, he reflected as he made his way home. She seems to specialize in surprises. Her whole presence is a glorious surprise.

13

Natana was very talkative as they drove to the airport. Philip suspected that she was perhaps nervous about letting their parting be too emotional. 'Glad to be going back?'

'Yes. Only I wish I could stay here too, in a way. But I'll be glad to get back to my own home and to Mme Marais.'

'You've missed her?'

'Yes. She's good for me. She has a good-humoured acerbity that is very salutary. And I'm sure she's missed me,' she added with naive realism.

'Who wouldn't?'

Natana ignored this. 'And I'll be so glad to get away from your English weather. Back to the sun and the dust and the shouting.'

'Shouting? Do you like that?'

'Very much! They shout about everything at home. About politics, about what they want, about what they have, about what they've done or are going to do, about what you've done or failed to do. Everything is turned into a drama. You go to market in the morning and there's sure to be some little incident or other, blown up into a great tragedy.'

'Such as?'

'An elderly woman walks up to the stall where they sell eggs. She has an egg in one hand, held out for all to see. The air is ringing with her lamentations and accusations as she marches up to the vendor. "*Regardez-moi donc cet oeuf!*"

she exclaims, pointing to a large crack in the shell. The vendor denies all responsibility. The egg was not cracked when she sold it. She does not sell cracked eggs. The injured party claims she's only just bought the egg, not five minutes ago. Corroboration from bystanders. There you are, says the vendor, five minutes! How long does it take to crack an egg? Chorus of approval from same bystanders. So it goes on.'

'And who wins?'

'Everybody wins. They all enjoy it thoroughly, and go home enriched by a little slice of high drama.'

'You must find us very dull here.'

'I do think you all have a tendency to take the edges off things. And it's the edges that sparkle. As far as I can see, a similar problem in this country would be tackled in a more private way, with hushed voices and no Greek chorus.'

Philip laughed. 'Oh, Natana, I shall miss you. And I see now how you must have missed all that, during these weeks you've been here. Have you been homesick?'

'I was during the first few weeks, before we established contact. It's been much better since. And even at my most miserable, I was sustained by the thought of why I was doing it.'

'For your mother?'

'Yes, and for you. If I've helped to give you a way back to her, even if it's only in the past, as you believe, then it's been worth it. I wouldn't have liked to go away with the feeling that I'd failed utterly.'

'You haven't failed at all. You've succeeded beyond all reasonable expectation. Please note the word "reasonable".'

'Yes, I get the message. If I've got you to the point of doing such an irrational thing as write to your dead wife, no matter what your expectations may be, then I must have made some sort of dent in your rationalist armour. And success, even a limited success, is much sweeter than failure. I don't think I can be very good at failing.'

'Lack of practice?' he suggested.

'Thank you. But seriously, remember you said something about Davina not being able to cope with failure? Well, I rather think I must be the same. I was so angry and generally upset yesterday, after my failed coup.'

'Yesterday. But not today. And that's the difference between you. She'll never let go of a failure. You have already. Here you are talking about it, examining it in a dispassionate way. That means you've survived it. And that's what this business of learning to love your mother is all about, isn't it? I've got to examine all those failures in our relationship, and let them go.'

'I'm so glad you're going to write to her. I think it's a brilliant idea.'

'We've Clive to thank for that. Funny how you can know someone so well and yet not know a thing like that. All those years, too, writing to Myra, without saying a word.'

'Why do you think he told you?'

'Because I'd told him of the task you'd set me, and I said I didn't even know how to begin. It was generous of him to tell me.'

'Yes, it was. Especially for a man like him.'

'What do you mean, a man like him?'

'He was quite aggressively rationalistic, very anti everything my mother's book stood for. And since that appears to be the view you both shared, it must have been difficult for him to admit to doing something that seemed so out of line.'

In the airport the shadow of their imminent parting suddenly fell over them, darkening their mood. Philip kept reminding himself of why Natana had come into his life, of how much he owed her, of how she had transformed his outlook on the past, and perhaps even the future. But at the same time there was a voice inside him shouting that he loved this girl, that he admired and desired her more than words could say, and that he was about to lose her.

Natana too was aware of a change in the emotional atmosphere, and interpreted it correctly. Several times, as they stood waiting in the queue, she was on the point of turning away and asking him to take her back to the flat. And because she was so aware of her longing to respond in this way to his desire, she stood silent beside him, apparently abstracted. For the last few days she had suspected that she was falling in love with Philip. She thought of Pierre in Perpignan, and dismissed the thought. That youth, that was all she could find in her heart to describe the young man she had mentioned to Philip as important to her. Now Philip seemed to take up her whole world, and she longed to give herself to him. She had to keep on reminding herself of her mission.

How could she help Philip to review the past, to reassess his relationship with her mother, to look beyond the bounds of the material world, if she was giving him the living, flesh-and-blood daughter to love at the same time? To yield to her own desires in the matter would be a complete betrayal of all she had set out to do.

They walked silently, side by side, up to the barrier where they must part. Not till the last moment did she turn her face to him.

'Oh, Natana!' he exclaimed, seeing her tears.

They clung to each other, while he gently kissed the tears on her cheek. Then they kissed full on the mouth, and the kiss was salt with her tears.

Philip never quite knew how he made his way back to the car park and found his own car. He never knew how long he sat there before he felt able to drive away, or how he managed to wend his way through the traffic back to his flat. He spent most of the day wandering about from one room to another, restless and miserable. His sense of loss was such that it struck him this was how people must feel after suffering a bereavement. He simply couldn't believe that the whole Natana episode had only lasted a few weeks, from the time of the appearance of the book till her departure that morning. And he had only actually known her for less than a week. Monday evening to Friday morning, he thought. It's impossible, it feels like a lifetime – a lifetime of joy and sorrow and guilt and, above all, surprise.

And the latest surprise was the story that her tears seemed to tell. Did she really care for him? Would she have been glad if he had bundled her back into the car and brought her here again? He had felt that he might have been able to persuade her. But the thought that she might have needed no persuading filled him with joy and despair. He blamed himself bitterly for his lack of decisiveness. Those tears and that kiss had told him what she wanted. Why had he let her go? If he had had the courage and the presence of mind to follow his desires – and hers, he added – they would both be here together. And once again he saw himself in bed with Natana, and cursed himself for not making it happen.

He had just emerged, jaded and guilty, from one of these voluptuous fantasies when he looked up and saw the row of photographs of Elise on the mantelpiece. Well, he thought, that's my answer. That's why neither of us could yield. He picked up one of the photos and took it over to the window. This time as he gazed at the beautiful, serene face, he was filled with more resentment than sorrow. Why did you send her, he was thinking, why did you send her, when you must stand between us all the time? And then he remembered that Elise had known nothing of Natana's mission. It was unfair to blame her for what had happened. Elise had meant to come herself and convert him.

Next he thought of how different mother and daughter were, in so many ways, and of the fact that what they had in common was precisely a system of beliefs that had been a stumbling block throughout the marriage. He had to admit to himself that his hostility to these beliefs had lessened considerably since Natana's arrival, and he wondered why she had proved so much more powerful an adversary than her mother.

And then he remembered the state of blissful acceptance and enhanced perception in which he had lived during his courtship and the early part of his marriage, and this brought him up with a powerful jolt. Might not the same have happened with Natana, had she stayed with him? Might the magic have faded, leaving only two people with diametrically opposed world views? He was reluctant to accept this idea. After all, he told himself, Natana has a much more dominating personality than Elise.

Having been reminded of the happiness of his first years with Elise, he thought of the fact that he had promised to try to love her again. A promise to Natana was something he considered sacred. He ought to start right now, and he'd been reminded of the best way to start, with the happy memories of the past. He took all the photographs and placed then carefully on his writing desk. Then he took out paper and pen and began writing.

'Dear Natana—' No, no, that's not it, he thought. And he scored out the word Natana and was about to replace it with her mother's name. But it seemed somehow indelicate to let her see where his thoughts had been running. He tore off the sheet and started again. Not that she would know, of course, but still . . . For his own sake, he couldn't afford to make a false start like that.

Dear Elise,

It's been a long time, and I don't know where to start. Not that it matters, of course, for you'll never see this. As Clive said, there's no divine postal service to get it to you. And there's no you to receive it. So where does that get us? The only possible, sensible answer is that it gets us nowhere. But perhaps the sensible answers aren't enough. I know that's what Natana would say. And it's also, of course, what you would have said. What, in fact, you did say, in all sorts of ways. In all sorts of intensely irritating ways, I may add.

Do you remember that time I lost the car keys and turned the house upside down looking for them? You said that was a silly way of going about it, and I said it was the only thing, therefore the sensible thing, to do. And after I had failed to find them you said you were going to do it your way and you sat down with that stupid little pendulum of yours and began asking it questions, and then you got up and went to the wardrobe and looked in the pocket of a jacket I had forgotten I was wearing the previous day, and there they were. Pure coincidence, of course, as anyone else would have admitted.

All right, it was you who found them. But there was a rational explanation, of course there was. You had subconsciously remembered that I was wearing that jacket, and sitting still while you played around with your pendulum had brought it back to you. And that's all it was, not, as you claimed, that the pendulum had answered your question.

Well, anyway, what I really meant to do was to recreate some of the wonderful moments we shared. That day we sat by the river, for instance, and felt as if we were flowing with it, in a smooth, tranquil movement that carried us gently into the future. And you said that the future and the present, and the past too, were all the same, and the magic was so powerful that I believed it too.

But you were wrong – we were wrong. The past, all our

past, has flowed away as irrevocably as the peaceful water that convinced us of this enticing untruth. And the proof is that you are now dead, and there is no way that we can communicate again, even though I am writing this letter. So why am I writing it?

For Natana's sake, of course. Because I promised Natana I'd try to love you again. But it's not easy. Even remembering the happy moments isn't all that much help. They lead so inevitably to all the arguments and misunderstandings with which we tormented each other.

Like the day I came home and found you in tears and you wouldn't tell me what was wrong, and then it turned out that you'd taken exception to something I'd said at breakfast – something about your mother being permanently lost in a Celtic mist. It wasn't all that insulting, after all. And besides, it was true.

Would you believe it, after you'd left me and I capitulated . . . (Please note, I did capitulate. I thought you'd gone to your mother's, so I didn't see any need to send out a search party, and yet I did phone after two days.) Anyway, when I phoned your parents and we discovered you were missing, your father told me that all she could do was sit with a pendulum in her hand, asking it to find you, while your father and I contacted the police.

And when you phoned soon after that, she claimed that it was because of the pendulum. Apparently it had sent a message through to you, and this was why you phoned. Did you get that message? Don't bother to reply, I know what the answer has to be.

As the days passed and the letter-writing progressed Philip noted with some dismay that he seemed to be dwelling on the bitter moments far more than on the happy ones. What he was really doing most of the time was simply carrying on the old arguments, giving his side of the story, justifying himself. And it was amazing how much he remembered – things that had lain buried in oblivion for years. And they all seemed to lead to the same, inescapable conclusion, that he was right and she was wrong.

Dear Elise,

This is the fifth consecutive day I've written to you, and so far everything leads to the same conclusion, that is, that I was right and you were wrong. I don't think it's really going to get us anywhere, do you? And since, for reasons beyond your control, you are necessarily barred from putting your side of the case, perhaps we could try doing it this way. Suppose I go over the same ground, trying to justify your viewpoint, putting it your way? I don't know that I'll be very good at it. Why not, I wonder? Lack of practice?

Do you know, it's just struck me, that I've been leading an extraordinarily narrowed existence, since you left, deliberately restricting myself to the company of those who shared my point of view, such as Clive and a few other friends. (To say nothing of my marriage to Davina!) So you can imagine the mindblowing, liberating effect of a visit from Natana.

Okay. Back to Lost Car Keys Drama. Over to you, Elise:

'Well, there he was, making all this fuss, turning everything upside down, emptying drawers . . . and you can guess who got the job of putting everything back in its place. And all this chaos and declamation in the service of what? Of doing things the sensible way. And it got him nowhere. All I did was sit down quietly and ask my pendulum a few questions. (By the way, I wonder whether he remembered this incident when he read my chapter on the use of the pendulum for finding mislaid objects or lost persons?) Well, as they say, the proof of the pudding . . . It was my way that found the keys. Not only did it prove successful, but it avoided all the physical chaos and mental disturbance that his method produced.'

Philip re-read that paragraph with mixed feelings. On the one hand he wanted to argue, to put his side of the case more effectively; on the other hand, he felt a certain satisfaction at having been able to cross over into enemy territory and describe the view from that side of the trenches.

Not bad, he murmured, not bad. I think Natana might be quite proud of me. Perhaps even Elise might approve. And for the first time it struck him that Elise's opinion was beginning to matter to him again. He put down his pen and looked at the row of Elises gazing back at him. He wondered whether he would ever be able to tell her that he had fallen in love with her daughter, that he had lusted after her, even in the midst of his mistaken belief that she was his own daughter. Ah, well, he thought, why shouldn't I write it? It's not as if she could ever get the letter. I can't shock her, I can't hurt her, for there's no Elise left to be shocked or hurt. No, not one of you, he said, looking at the row of Elises. Not one of you.

That evening Natana phoned. She missed him, she hoped he missed her, but not too much, and it was lovely to be back in the sun again.

'And the dust and the shouting?'

'Yes, they're lovely too. And Mme Marais, who tells me not to get too uppish just because I've found one reader for my mother's book.'

'Talking of which,' said Philip, 'I've started writing to her.'

'Yes, I know.'

'You *know*?'

'Yes,' said Natana. Then she added, quite casually. 'She told me.'

'She *told* you? How, might I ask?'

'She just sent me this conviction that you'd written. That's all. Nothing dramatic about it.'

'Just a perfectly ordinary, everyday form of communication!'

'I know you won't allow yourself to believe me. But the only alternative is that I'm lying to you. Would you rather believe that?'

'No, of course not. I know that's not the case, and you know I know it. But you could be deceiving yourself.'

'If that's what you'd rather believe, I don't mind. But keep writing, anyway. To Mummy, that is.'

'Not to you?'

'I'm a poor correspondent. I prefer to rely on the odd phone call.'

'I have to assume that this is how you contact your mother too.'

'You really do sound pretty sceptical today. I thought I was beginning to cure you.'

'Perhaps I'm missing my teacher.'

'You know what your teacher's instructions are.'

'To keep on writing?'

'Yes. Please, or I shall think I failed after all.'

'No, Natana, you mustn't think that. Never, never.'

After Natana had rung off Philip decided to obey her and write to Elise again. He remembered that he had come to the conclusion that there was no reason why he shouldn't write to the mother about his feelings for the daughter, since Elise would never know. Somehow he didn't feel quite so sure about that since the conversation with Natana. Not that there was anything in it, of course. But still, he thought he'd just leave that aspect of things for later. Plenty of other things to write about.

14

Dear Elise,

This is getting more and more difficult. It was hard enough, writing to you, knowing that there was no you to receive my letter. But now, what on earth am I to believe now, with Natana claiming that you've told her I'm writing? Don't you think you could make an effort and contact me directly? If you do exist, that is, which is of course impossible.

Anyway, whether you do exist or not, and whether I believe you do or not, is not the main point of the exercise. Natana's idea, and I'm sure it was the right one, was that I had to learn to love you again, for my own sake. So let's get back into the past once again and see how close we can get to each other.

And by the way, did you know that Natana brought me a rose the second day she came to see me? She said it was a quotation. I'm glad you told her about that. And I'm happy to say that I coped with it less ungraciously than on the first occasion. What a boor I must have been! Thank goodness you had the courage to risk a second rebuff!

Elise, do you realize what I've just written? For more than twenty years I've thought of our marriage as an almost unmitigated disaster. And yet now, for the first time, I've been able to accept the contrary view. For the first time I've accepted the fact that, in spite of all that went wrong, we did share a wonderful happiness for some time, and that this alone justifies the whole experience. If we had never met, my loss would have been immense. It has taken me more than twenty years, plus a visit from your turbulent and enchanting daughter, to see this. And now that I've been able to see it, perhaps I'll be able to write about our past without turning everything into an argument – with the right on my side, of course.

Now it seems perfectly reasonable that we had to have disagreements. It was bound to happen, with two people of such differing views. Why could we not just accept that this was the case, and take the good with the bad? Why did we (and I think we both did) insist that it was all to be perfect? Why did we let the bad bits overwhelm us so completely? Why did we let our happiness go, just because it wasn't absolute? As if anything in this world could be absolute!

And because we couldn't accept anything less than total happiness, we threw it all away. On the whole, I think you were luckier than I was. After we separated I had nothing to occupy me except licking my wounds, whereas you married a man who seemed able to give you all you needed. Merely looking at your photos makes that clear. You have kept your beauty, but you have grown. In comparison I feel stunted, dried up. Thank God you sent me Natana. Without her refreshing and revitalising presence, I think I'd have ended up as a handful of living dust.

Dear Elise,

Last night I dreamt about you. It's odd, that's the second time, recently. I suppose Natana told you (!) I'd had a dream about you the night before she turned up. Well, it happened again last night. This time I was at a funfair, and I was shooting at a target which consisted of one of your photos. And I got bull's eye, and your image disappeared and immediately popped up into position once again. And I shot again, and exactly the same thing happened. I don't know how often the performance was repeated. And I felt annoyed, even cheated, for I knew I deserved to win the prize, and yet I couldn't claim it, for there you were, in position. And at the same time, I can't explain how, I felt there was something good about it all. And I still can't explain it. Any ideas?

Yes, I know what you're going to say. I've been trying to shoot you dead for the last twenty odd years. And I thought I'd more or less succeeded. And the dream is telling me what Natana told me. The Elise who died in Perpignan some months ago is dead; but my Elise, the one who was a part of my life remains alive, for she was so much a part of me. And I can't kill her. So, however annoyed I may be about it, she, that Elise, remains alive, in spite of all my efforts, and I've got to take her into account. And that is where the feeling of goodness in the dream comes in. For I see now – and it took Natana to teach me – that I can only be whole by acknowledging this part of me, that loved you, and lived with you and, for some time, shared your crazy way of looking at the world.

Do you know, it hadn't struck me before, but since I lost the ability to see things your way, since I went back to my old, rationalist way of seeing the world, I have had not one moment of ecstasy. And you and I shared so many!

Do you remember the night we went out for a stroll when we were on holiday in Wales, staying in a tiny village? We left the village and its few street-lights behind, so we were able to see the stars – a rare occurrence for us city dwellers. And we spent an eternity leaning against a gate and looking at the stars and listening to the silence. And you told me you had seen angels in the sky, and I believed you, and tried to see them too. And although I never quite managed to see them I felt sure they were there. It was enough that you had seen them. I didn't see the angels, but I know I heard the music of the spheres.

And that is the kind of ecstasy I have never known since. And I had thought that I never could feel anything like that again after losing you. I have not known anyone else with whom I could share such a moment. Well, perhaps with Natana. But that's another story . . .

Dear Elise,

I forgot, I should have said this before. I really must congratulate you on your book. No, it hasn't convinced me – but I expect you know that, either directly or through Natana. But I must admit it's remarkably well written, very readable, and no doubt very convincing to anyone but a hardened unbeliever like me. And something else I should have done before now is thank you for taking the trouble to write it – no, more than that, I must thank you for even thinking of it, for wanting to do something for me. I don't mind admitting that this shows a magnanimity that – well, I was going to say that I didn't think you capable of. Which, I suppose, means that it shows a magnanimity of which I was (am?) quite incapable. But I think I'm learning.

Dear Elise,

Do you know, I think I am learning? I knew you had remarried, but I knew nothing about the marriage till Natana appeared. From her I learned that it had been a happy marriage, and my original reaction was simply to think that you had been luckier than I. A certain amount of envy, no doubt. And now, having heard more about Miquel from his daughter, having seen his photograph, and having seen his daughter, who is so like him, I find that the envy has gone, and I feel glad that he was able to give you the happiness I could only give you for so short a time.

And some day, perhaps, I'll tell you why I am so glad that Natana looks so like her father. But perhaps I don't need to tell you. Perhaps she has told you herself. Perhaps you have other means of knowing.

If so, then I must say I think you have an unfair advantage over the living. But I'm sure your sense of honour would keep you from any intrusive, voyeuristic prying into the hearts of us poor mortals. Can you imagine, Elise, can you imagine what an unfair advantage the dead would have over the living, if they were able not only to see our actions, but to read our thoughts? And that's a point, you see, that I feel entitled to make. Don't you think that the least any right-thinking spirit could do is make clear to us creatures, struggling on here below, what exactly are your powers? In short, how much do you know?

Because if you can read our thoughts and judge our fantasies, that puts you more or less on a level with the Almighty. As far as nuisance-value, goes, that is. And I don't like it, I must say, I just don't like it. As far as I am concerned, God can do as he pleases. I don't believe in him and have had no indications whatever of his existence. And a few weeks ago I would have been able to say exactly the same about the spirit world.

But now, having come across a number of what might be described as indications, I find my denial more difficult to maintain. It's not, of course, that I actually believe in your continued existence on another plane, but there are difficulties. I have to admit that there are difficulties. And I'm not helping matters, of course, with all this letter-writing. Behave *as if* something were the case for long enough and you end up believing in it.

Dear Elise,

I haven't written for several days, but it's not that I've not been thinking about you. In fact, it's precisely because my thoughts have been so taken up with you that I haven't written. Somehow, writing seems almost unnecessary. You're there all the time, looking at me, smiling at me, sometimes, I suspect, having a quiet little laugh at me. But with me, all the time with me.

Yesterday, for instance. Natana had phoned the previous evening, and I was feeling restless and slightly injured. Why must she insist on living in Perpignan, with that odd old stick of a Mme Marais? But whatever she does, and wherever she may choose to live, I'm sure it will be nowhere near here, and I know why and I expect you know why too. So we don't need to go into that.

Anyway, that's why I was feeling restless and slightly resentful. And I wanted to be with you – you see, Natana was right, you are my therapy. At first I thought I'd go back to one or other of the places where we had been so happy together. But then common sense intervened. I remembered that more than twenty years had passed, and that everything must be so changed that you and I simply wouldn't fit in. I decided to go somewhere I'd never been before, so that we could explore it together. So I drove out into the country and parked in a small village, and we spent a long time just wandering about the lanes.

And the ecstasy came back. Just looking at the fields and trees, and listening to the birds singing and the small things rustling in the hedge, and watching the clouds sailing across the sky, and smelling the earth – for it had rained a little earlier, the first rain after a long drought, and the earth smelt sweet and pungent and infinitely alive.

And you were with me.

Now I know this is impossible. But it should not be

impossible. If there is any justice, any justice whatever, the conviction I had that you were with me must be right. My Elise, the woman I knew and loved, was with me. This I insist on. It is a basic necessity, if I am to continue to live and grow, as opposed to merely existing in a state of arrested emotional development.

You have no doubt understood that I am trying to do a balancing act. By asserting that the Elise who was with me is only my Elise, who is, after all, nothing but a memory, I am leaving room for the statement that the real Elise is dead and buried and has ceased to exist in the material world, and therefore in any world, since no other exists.

Dishonest, do you think?

Perhaps. And yet . . . It's funny, but things seem to be going better in my world. For a long time I seemed to be at a standstill with my work. Nothing was turning out right. Routine work was boring and I seemed to have no new ideas coming to me. And now, within the last few days, it's all come alive again. It wouldn't be your doing, would it? Natana told me that at one time you had thought of learning something about physics, to try to bridge the gap between us. I just wonder whether you've been following a course in celestial physics up there. Do they have extramural classes in the Beyond? I don't suppose you'll tell me. Perhaps I'd better ask Natana. She seems to know rather a lot about both worlds.

Dear Elise,

As you know, Clive has been writing to Myra for over twenty years now. Do you think we'll go on as long? After all, why shouldn't we? I'm sure we have every bit as much to say to each other as they have. Even if only one of us is saying it . . .

15

Natana hadn't quite managed to recover the full flavour of life in Perpignan. It was lovely to be back, of course. It was good to be with Mme Marais again, and enjoy her quietly caustic remarks. And the sun shone as brightly as ever, and life was as varied and colourful, and the people as extroverted and entertaining as before. Well, nearly so. Natana thought of her remark to Philip about how the English seem to take the edge off things. Someone or something appeared to have taken much of the edge off life in Perpignan. There seemed to be appreciably less sparkle.

She had seen Pierre, she had even gone out with him. Once. That had been enough. He seemed so young, so gauche. Why had she not realized this before? When she got back from London she had intended going out with him regularly. She might even manage to fall in love with him, she had thought, hoping that this might act as an antidote to her persistent preoccupation with Philip. Now she realized that the whole idea was absurd. As if there could be any possible comparison!

She wasn't unhappy, of course. Nothing like that. Just perhaps a bit restless. And as the weeks passed she began to realize that there seemed to be some sort of interference in her communication with her mother. The line seemed to be dead. This had never happened before, and she didn't quite know what to make of it. Still less did she know what she could do about it.

Ever since her mother's death Natana had been convinced that a lot of her thoughts came to her directly from Elise. The sudden, inexplicable certainties – as when, for instance, she had felt convinced that Philip had started writing to his dead wife. The conviction had come hours before the telephone conversation in which Philip had mentioned that he was writing. This was one of the many examples of the sort of communication that she had come to take for granted. And now, suddenly, for no apparent reason, it had been withdrawn.

This interruption of contact with her mother left her feeling rather at a loss. She began to realize that a lot of her self-confidence and assurance came from the knowledge that all her life, both before and after her mother's death, Elise had always been there, available for consultation.

Yet for some weeks now there had been nothing. Nothing, in fact, since some time after Elise had let her know that Philip had started writing. Could it have anything to do with this? Was her mother too occupied with Philip to think of contacting her daughter? When this idea occurred to her she felt a sudden stab of two-pronged jealousy; a fear that Philip might prefer Elise, and that Elise might prefer Philip. And she, Natana, wanted to come first with both.

When she became aware of this sentiment she had to remind herself severely that a resumed form of communication between her mother and Philip was precisely what she had set out to achieve. It hadn't occurred to her, of course, before she set off on her mission, that their gain might in any way entail her loss. And, after all, why should it?

She gave some serious thought to the problem of this breakdown in communication. Did her mother perhaps realize how her daughter felt about Philip, and had this caused her to withdraw her approval? It must be something like that, she thought. And I know what Philip would say about it, anyway. Simply that I can no longer imagine that I'm in contact with her because my conscience isn't clear. And it's not clear because I know I've no right to be in love with Philip. He belongs to Mummy, or, failing that, to that bitch of a Davina.

Davina was having a hard time. She was suffering from loss of nerve. When the moment came to make the final move in her attempt at toppling the director of the company, she did nothing. For the first time in her life she let herself be swayed, not to say positively cowed, by caution. She simply hadn't had the courage to put her cards on the table, knowing that if she failed in the attempt she would lose everything. For how could she stay on in the firm when everybody would know how high she had aspired and therefore how great was her failure? Better to conceal her ambition than risk this loss of face. She had already done brilliantly, incredibly well. Why should she risk everything needlessly?

By the next day she had changed her mind, and wished she had made her attempt. But by then it was too late. She had lost her chance. She had muffed it, and had no one but herself to blame.

Basil didn't help matters. He knew what had happened, or rather, what hadn't happened, and seemed to take a malicious delight in proffering unwanted sympathy. From his point of view the present situation was perfectly satisfactory. If Davina had taken the risk, and won, there would certainly have been excellent pickings. If, however, she had lost and her chagrin and her pride had forced her to hand in her resignation, then things would have gone badly for Basil. Altogether it was just as well that the status quo should remain unaltered. So his sympathy flowed freely, like a stream of poisoned honey.

'I must say, I do admire you for having had the courage to do nothing. Doing nothing is by far the most difficult occupation in the world. So much easier to do something than to refrain. Fools rush in, and all that. But the really difficult thing is to do nothing.'

'You should know, at any rate. That's been your occupation all your life. And if it's all that difficult, you must be quite a hero.'

'I am, my dear, I am. Of the unsung variety. But it's you we were talking about, not me. I do admire your caution. A bird in the hand, as they say.'

'Who's gone all proverbial now? Fools rush in, bird in the hand, etc?'

'Ah, but I am not being proverbial on my own account. This is vicarious. I am merely exteriorizing your thoughts for you.'

'Kindly be good enough to leave my thoughts alone. I know exactly what they are. I don't need to be told. It might just turn out that it's you who has to be told what they are. And you might not like them all that much.'

Basil was used to some fairly harsh talk from Davina. He had a thick enough skin not to let it worry him. And he felt confident in his earlier assessment of the situation: that Davina was still too elated by the thought of being the mistress of an aristocrat, even of so dog-eared a variety, to think of doing without the kudos this brought her. Again he told himself she was good for another few months at least, and returned to the delightful occupation of Davina-baiting.

Philip, in the midst of his epistolary frenzy, suddenly experienced an unaccountable sensation of let-down. It was all too one-way. He longed for some sort of response. But that, of course, was quite out of the question. Elise would not and could not write back.

Why am I doing this? he asked himself. Wasting paper. Wasting trees. Natana should have thought of that, she's so ecology-conscious. Wasting paper, wasting time. That's all I'm doing.

Then his sense of fairness took over, and he decided that neither the time nor the paper had been wasted. He had learned a lot from the letters. Elise, his Elise, had come alive again in his mind, and they were closer now than they had been since their paths had begun to diverge after the first year or two of marriage.

And Natana had been right. The reconciliation had brought healing with it. He had felt refreshed and strengthened. His renewed contact with Elise – well, with the memory of Elise – had restored his sense of values and his sense of wonder. Life was certainly far more worth living than it had been for many years. Simply writing the letters had taught him to look into himself, to try and see where he had gone wrong instead of surrounding himself by an impregnable barrier of self-justification. Yes, the experiment had been well worth doing.

But now? Was it perhaps time to stop? Since there was nothing coming from the other side, since there never could be anything coming from the other side . . . Or was he going to be like Clive, and spend the rest of his life writing letters to a dead woman?

'By the way, Clive, are you still writing to Myra?'

'Of course. It's become part of my daily pattern. I don't think I could stop. Are you still writing to Elise?'

'Yes. I mean, I think so. Only . . . '

'Only what?'

'Don't you get a bit frustrated by the fact that there's never any reply?'

'No, not really. After all, I'm not expecting one. The frustration comes when you are expecting a letter that doesn't turn up.'

'I wish I could see it that way. When you write a letter to someone, you expect some sort of feedback. Something to reply to. Do you mean to say that you don't really mind not getting an answer?'

Clive thought for a moment. 'I did at first. I minded terribly. But now . . . No, I don't really think that not having a reply bothers me all that much. I suppose what I'm doing really is writing a sort of diary.'

'Exactly. It's got to be that, or frustration. It seems there's no middle way. And I don't really want to write a diary. On the other hand, I promised Natana . . . '

'That you'd go on writing for ever?'

'No. Nothing was said about the timescale.'

'What was it, after all, that Natana wanted you to do?'

'She wanted me to learn to love Elise again. And I have. It's a bit like having a picture restored. All the grime of my resentment has been washed away, and I can see her as she was, lovely and lovable. It's a great liberation.'

'My motivation was quite different from yours. No grime to wash away. And if you've achieved what you set out to do, then perhaps you don't need to write any more.'

Philip nodded. 'I think I'll give it a rest.'

So he stopped writing. And the frustration of not getting a reply was replaced by a sense of emptiness and restlessness. He felt that now that he'd got over his hang-ups about the past, he should have something more to fill his life than the meagre routine he had lived with for so long. What I need, he thought, is a little human contact. Apart from Clive, there's no one, really.

The human contact that he would have liked, of course, was Natana. But, deprived of the magic of her presence, he had gradually come round to the view that seeing Natana again might prove disastrous for both of them. It would almost certainly be a repetition of what had happened with her mother. The attraction was as great, and the problems were identical; and in addition he had to face the unpalatable and inescapable fact that there was a gap of nearly thirty years between them.

No, Natana had been right, absolutely right, to go away when she did. He hoped she was happy with her young man in Perpignan. It was a slightly grudging hope, but he tried to make it as sincere as possible.

So, Natana was out. But now that she had extracted him from the emotional impasse he had been living in for so long, he really must give some thought to the matter and find some way of relating to a few more members of the human race. Should he perhaps join some club? Never in his adult life had he felt the slightest inclination to join any kind of society. He just wasn't gregarious enough. Still, he must find something to fill the space left by not writing to Elise. He felt he couldn't go back to the emptiness of his pre-Natana existence. Not now that he had emerged from his carapace of self-imposed indifference.

'I think I'll go and spend a few weeks with the Laplaces,' Natana announced one morning early in September.

Mme Marais looked up and smiled.

'Yes, that's a good idea. Paris will blow some of the cobwebs away.'

'Cobwebs?'

'You have been rather like the weather lately. Just a little *maussade*.'

This home truth came as a bit of a surprise to Natana. She thought she had been very skilful in concealing the underlying glumness of her mood. It served to confirm her in her intention. She would go and spend some time with the Laplaces. Up till recently this family had always spent the summer in the house next to theirs, and the children had played together. Now they were all grown up, and came less frequently. But the friendship was as strong as ever, and Natana was in the habit of spending a few weeks with them in Paris every now and then.

She was happy to see her friends again. Edmond, the eldest son, who had been working abroad for some years, had just come home.

'Are you going to settle in Paris now?' she asked him.

'I don't know what I'm going to do. I've got a job waiting for me here, but I'm not sure that I want it now.'

'Why on earth not?' Natana was looking at him in concern, sensing the unhappiness behind his indecision.

'Well, I came back to get married – to Caroline – remember her?'

'Of course! Such a nice girl.'

'I'm not so sure about that. The very day I arrived she told me she's marrying someone else next week.'

'Oh, Edmond, I'm so sorry.' Natana put her hand on his arm and looked at him out of tear-filled eyes.

They spent a lot of time together after that, more or less discovering each other. The five-year age gap between them had meant that Edmond had always stood rather apart, while Natana had played with his younger brothers and sisters, her contemporaries.

It didn't take her long to find out where Edmond would probably be more than willing to find consolation for his disappointment. And if it hadn't been for Philip . . .

Davina was beginning to suspect that Basil didn't really know his place. He was rather too free with his little barbed comments. And there was altogether too much French in his conversation. She knew perfectly well that he realized she was not at home in this language. At school she had specialised in maths and science, and her French was very rudimentary. Basil's insistence on peppering his speech with it was beginning to get on her nerves. At first she had merely assumed he was simply doing it out of habit, because that was the way his family and friends spoke. But by now she had come to see he was using it as a weapon. It made her feel small, this reminder of the fact that his social sphere was so much higher than hers. In addition, she was sure he was deliberately doing this because he knew she had difficulty in understanding these elegant little morsels of speech. And if there was anything Davina couldn't stand, it was the frustration of not understanding. This bothered her even more than the humiliation of having her ignorance exposed.

'You look rather less than enthusiastic today, *mon ange*.'

'Today? I don't know that today's any worse than any other day. And it certainly isn't any better. I'm just tired of today. And that's all there ever seems to be. Just one today after another.'

'Ah, there, you see, we differ. I'm a great lover of todays. *Le vierge, le vivace et le bel aujourd'hui*, as the poet says. Mallarmé, of course. But I'm sure you recognized the quotation.'

Without saying anything Davina got up and went over to the desk by the window. A moment later she came back to the centre of the room and handed Basil a cheque.

'There you are.'

'But, *mon petit chat*, it's not the end of the month yet.'

Davina stood looking at him in silence, with an ironic smile on her face.

With some misgiving Basil looked at the cheque and then started up from the couch.

'But, but . . . *mon petit chou*, this is twice the normal amount.'

'I believe that is standard practice. In lieu of a month's notice. You can start packing right away.'

Basil's pale features had turned scarlet. 'Bitch!' he said as he walked out of the room, pocketing the cheque. He knew his Davina too well to think of trying to mollify her.

Natana dialled the Laplace phone number and waited for a reply, hoping it wouldn't be Edmond—

'Oh! Edmond, it's you. I'm just phoning to say I'm on my way to London, and would you mind telling your mother?' She had just realized this was Saturday, and that Philip would be at home. Suddenly it had struck her that she must go and see him at once. To clarify the situation, as she put it to herself.

'London?' Edmond sounded shocked. 'You never said a thing about going to London when you left the house this morning.'

'I know, I know. I hadn't thought of it then. I haven't even got a toothbrush with me. It's just a *coup de tête*, if you like. But I've some unfinished business in London, and I thought I'd better get it settled before . . . before . . . '

'A man, I suppose?'

'Yes, of course, a man. What else?'

She heard a sigh coming to her across half of Paris.

'So would you please tell your mother I may be back in a few days. Or not.'

'If it's not a few days, when will it be?'

'I really don't know, Edmond. It all depends.'

'On what?'

'Well, not on me.'

Soon she would be climbing the stairs of Philip's flat once again, remembering the nervousness with which she had climbed them on her first few visits, before she had actually met him. How different this time! This time she had no doubts about the welcome she would get.

Everything else was uncertain. She just didn't know how things would go. She was prepared to find that it didn't work out. In a few days she might be back on her way to Paris, and perhaps that would be the best thing in the long run. Best for her and certainly best for Edmond, she felt pretty sure. But, whatever the outcome, she would not be going back unsettled and unsatisfied, as the last time. She would at least have a few days with Philip – and a few nights with Philip. After that, if need be, she would relinquish him to her mother. Any sense of disloyalty she might have felt about what she was doing was cancelled by her mother's silence. Since Elise seemed to have written her off, then she would just have to make her own decisions, wouldn't she?

Well, she had made her decision. And she wasn't going to be put off by any scruples on Philip's part, either. Thinking of their parting kiss at the airport – tender, passionate, filled with longing, tasting of tears, she imagined herself in Philip's flat once more; in his arms, and this kiss would be like the other one, but without the tears. The tears might come later – would come, if they decided to part in the long run. But this kiss, at least, would not remain unfulfilled.

Philip was sitting at home trying to cope with the problem of what to do about the emptiness in his life. None of the solutions he had come up with seemed to be solutions at all, when properly examined. In the end he decided that what they all had in common was the fact that none of them really committed him to anything. You join a club, and if you don't like it, you drop out. And then you join another, and the same thing happens again. And so you keep on floating. Getting nowhere. Edging your way round difficulties instead of tackling them.

He was smiling wryly over the discovery that the problem with his life was that he hadn't enough problems – when he heard the bell ring. Clive? Who else could it be? There was no one else who could conceivably be ringing his bell unannounced. Not now that Natana had gone.

He opened the door.

Davina stood there, carrying a weekend bag.

'Oh, my God!' said Philip.

'Nice of you to put it that way.'

Davina stepped inside and put her bag down on the hall floor.

Philip closed the door.

They stared at each other in silence for a moment.

'Ten years,' said Davina.

'Doesn't look like it,' he said, impressed by her youthful appearance. 'You haven't changed.'

'I was rather hoping that we both had, just a little. Just enough to be able to stand each other's company.'

'And you're thinking of moving in?' he asked, nodding at the bag on the floor.

'You might be able to talk me into it.'

Philip was reminded of one of the qualities he had found so attractive in Davina, the light, ironic touch she often gave to her conversation.

'I might try,' he conceded, 'if you twist my arm.'

Three days later Natana stood waiting, expectant, almost exultant.

The door was opened and she found herself staring at Davina. The shock was so great that she was unable to do anything to conceal it.

'We weren't expecting you.'

The dismay on Natana's face, as she took in the full implications of the word 'we', told her story so clearly that Davina felt she had no need to be bitchy. She, after all, was in possession.

'You'd better come in,' she said, and there was none of the usual irony in her voice. 'Philip!' she called. 'We have a visitor. You can take Natana through to the sitting room. I'll make some coffee.'

Philip and Natana stared at each other in agonised silence. Then he led her to the sitting room.

As soon as Philip had closed the door and sat down opposite Natana she asked, 'Does she . . . Is she . . . ?'

'Staying here, you mean? Well, yes, sort of . . . That is, she arrived three days ago, out of the blue. She'd just thrown out that effete aristocrat.'

'And – is this to be a permanent arrangement?'

'We've given ourselves a week to find out.'

Natana had recovered sufficiently to see the irony of the situation.

'And I suppose this is all my doing, isn't it? If I hadn't gone to see her . . . '

'She might not have thought of coming? Exactly.'

'They say success is sweet. I suppose I'll have to try and enjoy this one.' Natana knew she was going to shed many bitter tears over this particular success, but she was determined not to let Philip see any of them.

'You might have told me,' she remarked.

'I did. Or rather, I tried. I phoned the very evening Davina appeared, but got no reply. So I then wrote. I've done my best to keep you in the picture.'

Natana nodded. 'I've been away, staying with friends in Paris. And Mme Marais is away too.'

So far Philip had been too embarrassed by the situation to

be able to do more than answer Natana's questions. Now he managed to say something that he hoped would lessen the bitterness of the moment for the girl.

'It's not an ideal arrangement. You know what I really wanted. What we both wanted, I think.'

Natana nodded.

'But, in an odd way, the very fact that it isn't ideal means that it might just work. I know that sounds paradoxical, but then you like paradox, don't you? The fact is that, since learning to love your mother again, for which I must be eternally grateful to you, I've learned a lot. And one of the things I've learned is that I've spent my life trying to make things too easy for myself.'

Natana permitted herself one malicious observation.

'In that case, you seem to have made a good choice.'

At this point Davina came back with the coffee.

'After all, it's what you wanted, isn't it? This situation, I mean,' she said.

Natana nodded.

'Sugar?'

'Two, please. It's the right thing, when you're in shock, isn't it?'

They all laughed, and Philip got up and kissed her on the forehead.

'Natana, you're wonderful. Inimitable.'

Later on Natana reflected that this kiss had been so completely different from the one she had been expecting; and yet it had brought her some comfort in its way. It had shown that Philip still loved and admired her, and that he was not going to be entirely dominated by Davina.

'Philip tells me you've thrown out your aristocratic companion. Was he really an earl's brother?'

'Yes. Perfectly genuine.'

'I thought he was rather nice.'

'Basil,' stated Davina in an unimpassioned voice, 'is a bastard of the first water.'

Conversation flagged after that, and Natana didn't stay much longer.

After she had gone Davina turned to Philip and said, 'That young woman has a lot to thank me for.'

Philip looked at her ruefully.

'I suppose I have too. I've no doubt it would have been a disaster for us both. But I wouldn't say that thankfulness seemed her predominant emotion, would you?'

'Not just yet. But she struck me as fairly resilient. She'll bounce back.'

Natana would have liked to wander through the slums Philip had described. They would have fitted her mood, as they had fitted his on that occasion. But she had no idea of how to find them. Of course, she could always hail a cab and ask the driver to take her to some slums. In spite of her misery she managed a weak smile at the thought of his probable reaction to such a request.

Instead of slums she had to make do with the Embankment, where she spent an hour leaning against the cold parapet, looking at the dirty water and weeping freely.

'You all right, dear?'

A middle-aged lady was standing beside her, looking at her with a mixture of concern and curiosity.

'Yes thanks, I'm fine,' sniffed Natana, unconvincingly.

'Nothing wrong with a good cry, dear. Does you good, I always say. I just wish you wouldn't stand there to do it. Might give you ideas, it might.'

'Oh! I hadn't thought of that. No, really, that's not what I was thinking of at all. And thank you for your concern.'

To prove there really were no suicidal thoughts in her

mind she dried her tears and asked the woman what was the quickest way to the airport.

If she hurried she would be able to get back to Paris that evening. It might be pretty late when she arrived, but she would phone Edmond and ask him to come and meet her. He would be delighted.

And, presumably, so would her mother. That too would be a comfort. Now that she had been forced to abandon her dream of being united with Philip, she felt sure that communication with her would be resumed. Besides, Elise had always been very fond of Edmond. She would be happy to welcome him. And Edmond needed help. Natana gave a little sigh of content, pleased to have a mission in life again. For the first time in months she felt undivided.

As the plane took off she fixed her eyes on a distant patch of blue surrounded by white fleecy clouds. In a moment it disappeared, and they were flying through dense, swirling mist.

She saw this as a metaphor for what her life had been over the past few months. Making a characteristic effort to look forward, instead of back, she fixed her mind on the immediate future. In another hour she would be back in Paris, and she would phone Edmond.

And he would come at once.

Suddenly, dazzlingly, they were clear of the cloud, flying steadily through a sea of blue, with the level rays of the evening sun streaming across from the west.

Natana smiled and settled back in her seat, relaxed. Once again she could see where she was going.